Henry D. Harrower

Captain Glazier and His Lake

Henry D. Harrower

Captain Glazier and His Lake

ISBN/EAN: 9783337183592

Printed in Europe, USA, Canada, Australia, Japan

Cover: Foto ©Andreas Hilbeck / pixelio.de

More available books at **www.hansebooks.com**

AND

HIS LAKE

An Inquiry

INTO THE HISTORY AND PROGRESS OF EXPLORATION AT THE
HEAD-WATERS OF THE MISSISSIPPI SINCE THE
DISCOVERY OF LAKE ITASCA

IVISON, BLAKEMAN, TAYLOR & COMPANY
NEW YORK AND CHICAGO

_1 8~ ~_

NOTE.

The preparation of this paper was originally begun with a view to its publication in the issue of the "Educational Reporter" for June, 1886. Its purpose was to state what was known about the head-waters of the Mississippi, and briefly to inquire into the validity of the claims of Captain Willard Glazier to having made important discoveries and explorations in that region.

In common with many others who have editorial supervision of geographical and educational publications, I had been frequently urged to recognize these claims of Captain Glazier ; but this inquiry soon assumed such proportions that I contented myself with publishing an extract from Nicollet's report of his explorations in 1836, together with a brief reference to Captain Glazier. With such a statement of previous exploration, it was hoped that Captain Glazier and his friends would somewhat modify or moderate their claims in his behalf. The very opposite has seemed to be the effect, if one may judge correctly from the extracts from the newspaper press which have been sent to me during the past three months.

As a result what was first intended to be a brief inquiry into the history and progress of exploration at the head-waters of the Mississippi becomes, by force of circumstances, rather the exposure of an attempted fraud which has been altogether too successful for the credit of American intelligence and scholarship. Yet it is always far more agreeable to gather together the scattered data that go to make up the sum of knowledge in any field than simply to break down a reputation for knowledge, however fraudulent that reputation may be ; and so I have taken far greater pleasure in collecting under one cover the few facts relative to the exploration of the sources of the great river since the white man first sighted Lake Itasca, than in any pillorying of Captain Glazier, however effective that may seem to be.

HENRY D. HARROWER.

NEW YORK, *October*, 1886.

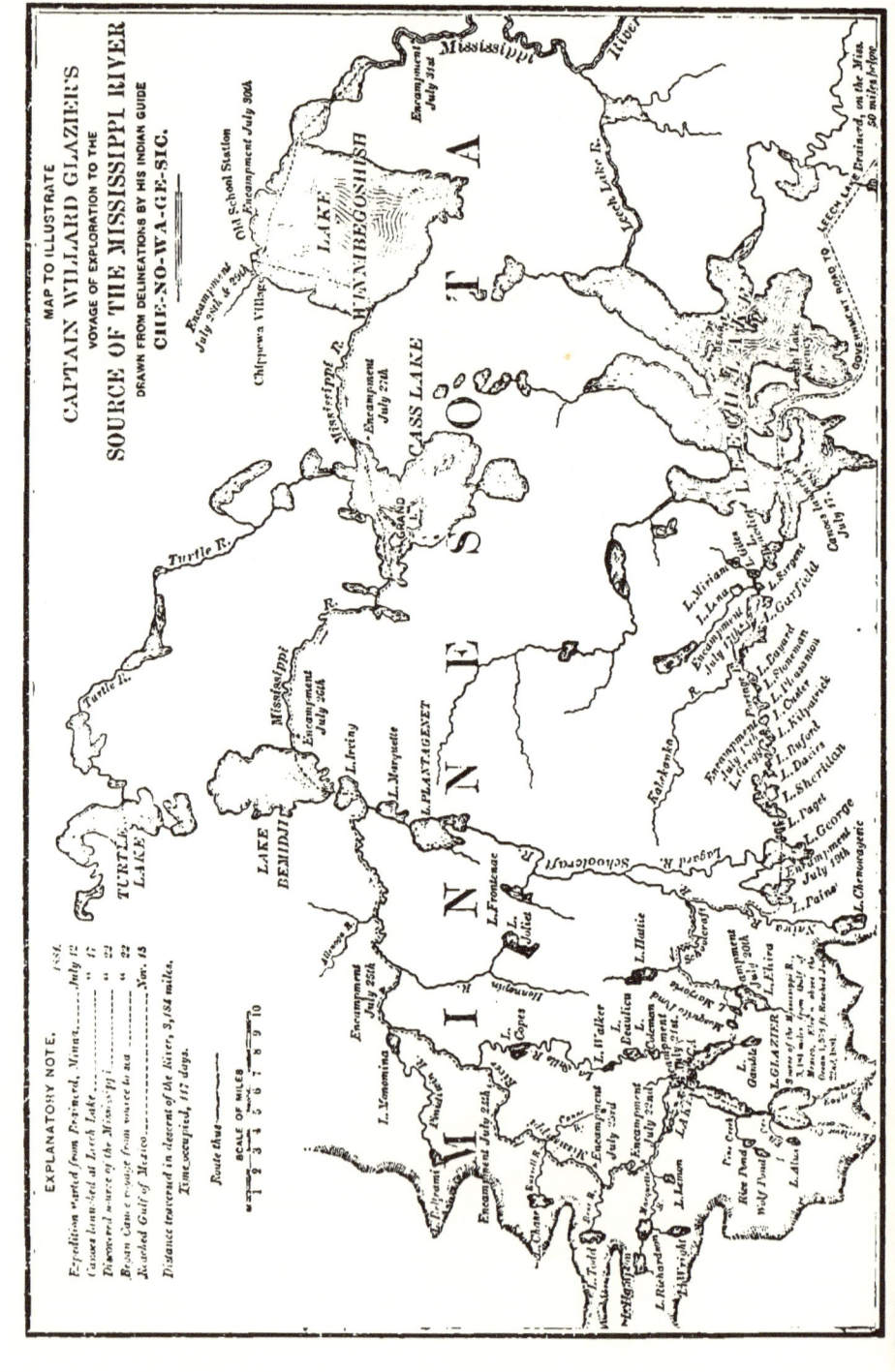

MAP TO ILLUSTRATE
CAPTAIN WILLARD GLAZIER'S
VOYAGE OF EXPLORATION TO THE
SOURCE OF THE MISSISSIPPI RIVER
DRAWN FROM DELINEATIONS BY HIS INDIAN GUIDE
CHE-NO-WA-GE-SIC.

EXPLANATORY NOTE.   1881.

Expedition started from Brainerd, Minn.......July 12
Canoes launched at Leech Lake................ "   16
Discovered source of the Mississippi......... "   22
Brown Came e voyage from source to sea........ "   22
Reached Gulf of Mexico....................... Nov. 13

Distance traversed in descent of the River, 3,184 miles,
Time occupied, 117 days.

Route thus _____

SCALE OF MILES
1 2 3 4 5 6 7 8 9 10

Captain Glazier and His Lake.

According to the latest version of modern burlesque, the King of Spain once upon a time said to Columbus, " Columbus, can you discover America?"

To which replied the great Christopher: "Certainly, your majesty, if you will give me a ship."

So the king gave him a ship, and he sailed and he sailed until he came in sight of land. Sailing up to the shore, he hailed a chief and asked him, " Is this America?"

Whereupon the chief, turning to his band, said: " There is no use of denying it; we are discovered;" and, addressing himself to Columbus, owned up: " Yes, this is America. Who are you?"

" I am Columbus."

" Why, of course; I might have known it."

Very much the same way, a few years ago Captain Willard Glazier propounded to himself (for he acknowledged no kinglier) thus: "Captain, can you discover Lake Glazier, the true source of the Mississippi River?"

"Of course I can, if I can have a canoe and a few trusty friends who will go with me into the wilds of Minnesota."

So they went forth into the northern wilds; and after a time they came to a lake, and they voted that it was Lake Glazier, and that no white man had ever seen it before, and that Captain Glazier was a great discoverer. And thus he won eternal fame by the unanimous vote of five of his fellow-citizens, including three "Indians, not taxed."

THE GREAT DISCOVERY.

Captain Glazier is a gentleman who belonged to the Union volunteer army in the civil war, and there is no reason to doubt that he was a faithful and gallant soldier. Since the war he has been a rather voluminous writer of war reminiscences, in which Captain Glazier generally figures as the leading character and hero, he has traveled across the continent on horseback from Boston to San Francisco, and has made a canoe trip from the head-waters of the Mississippi to the Gulf of Mexico.

It is in connection with this trip down the Mississippi that Captain Glazier claims to have carved his name on the very cap-stone of American geographical research. He tells us * that while crossing the continent on horseback in 1876 he came to the Mississippi River, and, musing on that mighty stream and "the uncertainty that existed as to its true source," he concluded "that there was yet a rich field for exploration in the wilds of Minnesota." In course of time, therefore, we find Captain Glazier ready to enter upon the exploration of this rich field. There is no evidence that Captain Glazier made any effort to inform himself as to what was already known about the sources of the river. He certainly took no account of the data in possession of the government Land Department, and generally he proceeded on the theory that everybody was as ignorant as he in regard to the matter.

Accordingly, in the month of May, 1881, he sets out with two companions for the North-west. He goes to St. Paul, Minn., thence to Brainerd, and on across the Chippewa Indian Reservation to Leech Lake, where he finds Indian guides for the rest of the journey. Having provided himself with canoes, guides, and interpreter, the party now numbering six in all, he goes by water and numerous portages to Lake Itasca, and begins the exploration of its feeders to find "the true source of the Mississippi." Having found one of the largest inlets of Itasca, the party follows it to an expansion in a small lake, of which they proceed to take possession in the name of Captain Glazier. As they sail across the lake, a deer is seen standing on the shore and an eagle sweeps approvingly over their heads—fit omen of immortal fame. Captain Glazier then calls his audience to order at the foot of a promontory overlooking the lake, and delivers to them an address upon the greatness of their

---

* "The Recent Discovery of the True Source of the Mississippi River," by Willard Glazier, "American Meteorological Journal," 1884, vol. i., p. 176. Also, "Sword and Pen: or, Ventures and Adventures of Willard Glazier." By John Algernon Owens. Philadelphia: P. W. Ziegler & Co., 1884, p. 438.

own achievements, generously explaining and excusing the failures of their distinguished predecessors in the work of Mississippi River exploration. A volley from their firearms is fired in honor of each member of the party, and one of his white companions gives the captain a "surprise," by proposing " that the newly-discovered lake be named Lake Glazier, in honor of its discoverer. The proposition was seconded by Moses Lagard, the interpreter, and carried by acclamation." * Then Che-no-wa-ge-sic, the chief guide, assumes an oratorical attitude, and addresses the captain in a few words of true Indian eloquence. " The Indians chimed in with a Chippewa yell, and then, while the air was still reverberating with the sound of their voices, they all paused to take in once more the scene of their explorations." †

The party returns to Schoolcraft Island, in Lake Itasca, where Captain Glazier's companions draw up a petition in due form, addressed " To Geographical Societies," in which they state the nature of the discovery, claim the privilege of naming the lake " Lake Glazier, in honor of the leader of the expedition, whose energy, perseverance, and pluck " carried them through their undertaking, and earnestly " petition all geographical societies to give it that prominence which has heretofore been accorded to Lake Itasca, and to which it is justly entitled as the primal reservoir of the grandest river on this continent." This petition was duly signed by all the party *except Captain Glazier,* ‡ and reads as follows :

" Schoolcraft's Island, {
" Lake Itasca, *July* 22, 1881. }

" To Geographical Societies :

" We, the undersigned companions of Captain Willard Glazier, in his voyage of exploration to the head-waters of the Mississippi, are fully convinced that the lake discovered by him, and claimed as the head of the river, is beyond question the source of the ' Father of Waters.'

" The privilege of bestowing a name upon the new discovery having been delegated to us, we hereby name it Lake Glazier, in honor of the leader of the expedition, whose energy, perseverance, and pluck carried us through many

---

* It is gratifying to know that there were no negative votes recorded against the proposition.

† " Sword and Pen," p. 475.

‡ " Sword and Pen," pp. 503, 504. It is worth while to reproduce this quite exceptional document entire, if for no other purpose, at least to preserve the names of a remarkable coterie of *savants.*

difficulties, and brought us at last to the shores of this beautiful lake, which is the true source of the great river.

"We earnestly petition all Geographical Societies to give it that prominence which has heretofore been accorded to Lake Itasca, and to which it is justly entitled as the primal reservoir of the grandest river on this continent.

[*Signed*]

" BARTLETT CHANNING PAINE, Indianapolis, Indiana, GEORGE HERBERT GLAZIER, Chicago, Illinois,	White Companions.
MOSES LAGARD, CHE-NO-WA-GE-SIC, SEBASTINE LAGARD, Leech Lake, Minnesota,	Interpreter and Indian Guides."

FROM THE SOURCE TO THE GULF.

Captain Glazier is now ready to begin his descent of the stream, "for, as yet, but a small portion of his tremendous undertaking has been accomplished." The rest is to make his canoe voyage to the Gulf of Mexico, and "to deliver a lecture on the way at every town of importance, on both banks, as he floats down the stream." He also undertakes to interview newspapers and to instruct geographical and historical societies in regard to his great discoveries. The newspapers respond with avidity, and he is everywhere warmly hailed and welcomed by expressions "such as would naturally occur in a country where the people delight to honor enterprise, courage, and ambition." The people everywhere flocked to the landing-places to do him honor; and "many, more impatient than the rest, would put out in canoes and skiffs to meet him on the way. Upon disembarking, he would be escorted to his hotel, usually preceded by a band playing 'Hail to the Chief,' 'See the Conquering Hero Comes,' or other appropriate airs, and wherever he delivered his lectures large audiences greeted him, curious to see and hear the man who had at last discovered the source of the Mississippi." *

And so on down the great river till Port Eads is reached, where, amid the booming of guns and the waving of flags, they paddle out into the wide expanse of the Gulf. "He was proud of the fact that he was the first to stand at the fountain-head of his country's grandest river and was the first to trav-

---

* "Sword and Pen," p. 483.

erse its entire course . . . and now at its outlet could write *finis* to the great work of his life. Few men in the world can say as much, for the energy, perseverance, unfaltering will, and indomitable courage which characterize Captain Glazier are of rare occurrence, and entitle him to a foremost position in the ranks of America's distinguished sons." *

GLORY GALORE.

This certainly is glory galore, and Captain Glazier seems to revel in the greatness of his name and renown. His biographer, who seems to know his inmost thoughts, and to be indeed his other self, dwells with admiring phrases upon his wonderful achievements and his sure title to eternal fame. And the captain seems to have been able to impress large numbers of people with this estimate of himself.

Upon the return of Captain Glazier to New Orleans the mayor of that city tendered him the freedom of the city, and the New Orleans Academy of Sciences gave him a public reception, at which resolutions were passed recognizing the great results of his expedition. Dr. J. S. Copes,† the president, in the name of the academy, thanked Captain Glazier, and congratulated him upon his contribution to American geographical knowledge,

---

* " Sword and Pen," p. 489.

† The following copy of an autograph letter from Dr. Copes indicates how thoroughly Captain Glazier had impressed himself upon that eminent gentleman :

" CAPTAIN GLAZIER:—I congratulate you upon the successful completion of your search for the primal reservoir of the Mississippi River. It would be well for the country to erect before the view of its youths and all young men two monuments, three thousand miles asunder—the one at the source, the other at the mouth, of the great river of North America—upon which should be chiseled ' Enterprise, Courage, Faith, Fortitude, Patriotism, Philanthropy,' leaving to posterity the selection of an illustrative name to be engraven on each one when events shall have pointed conclusively to the benefactor most worthy of this honor. With great respect, yours very truly,

" J. S. COPES,
" President New Orleans Academy of Sciences.

" NEW ORLEANS, *Nov.* 19, 1881."

Whatever thought may have been in Dr. Copes's mind, it is safe to say that the name of Glazier will never be engraven on either of the monuments which he proposes to rear in honor of Enterprise, Courage, Faith, Fortitude, Patriotism, and Philanthropy.

comparing him with De Soto, Marquette, La Salle, Hennepin, and Joliet. They had explored only sections of the great river, "while Captain Glazier *had made the important discovery of its primal reservoir*, and traversed its entire length to the sea."

From New Orleans Captain Glazier proceeded to St. Louis, where, on the evening of January 14, 1882, he addressed a large audience, consisting of members of the Missouri Historical Society, the Academy of Sciences, clergy, officers and teachers of the public schools, assembled at the Mercantile Library Hall. He was introduced by Judge Albert Todd, an eminent lawyer and Vice-President of the Historical Society, who compared him with the whole line of explorers from Jason to Stanley. "Impelled by this spirit of enterprise in search of truth," thus said Judge Todd, "Captain Glazier has discovered, at last, the true source of our grand and peerless river, the Father of Waters." *

LITERARY WORK.

Subsequent to these events Captain Glazier naturally rested for a time on his laurels and devoted himself to "literary work." Soon, however, he took the proper means of communicating his discoveries to various learned bodies, seeking the recognition due his labors and achievements. He published an elaborate map of the head-waters of the Mississippi, showing the location of Lake Glazier. This he sent to Judge Daly, the distinguished and versatile President of the American Geographical Society; and a

---

* "Sword and Pen," pp. 497, 498. Like Dr. Copes, Judge Todd seems to have taken Captain Glazier at his own estimate, and to have accepted his story of his exploits and discoveries without a grain of allowance. The following pleasing souvenir is reproduced by the author of "Sword and Pen," as showing an "especial appreciation of the captain's endeavor to increase the geographical lore of the Mississippi River:"

"To CAPTAIN WILLARD GLAZIER—*Greeting:*
    "With triple wreaths doth fame thine head now crown;
    The patriot soldier's, in fierce battles won;
    The 'Pen's' than the 'Sword's' mankind's greater boon;
    The bold Explorer's finding where was born
    The Rivers' King, till now, like Nile's, unknown.
    May years of high emprise increase thy fame,
    And with thy death arise a deathless name.
                "ALBERT TODD,
        "Vice-President Missouri Historical Society.
"ST. LOUIS, *Jan.* 14, 1882."

copy of the map, with Captain Glazier's letter, was transmitted by Judge Daly to the "New York Herald" in June, 1884, and thus given to the world with the stamp of approval of the greatest geographical authority in America.

In 1884 he contributed to the pages of the "American Meteorological Journal" an elaborate account of the "Recent Discovery of the True Source of the Mississippi River," illustrated with maps and engravings, and this had wide circulation, with the apparent approval of a scientific journal edited by a distinguished member of the faculty of the University of Michigan. The same year appeared a book of over five hundred pages, to which reference has been made above— "Sword and Pen; or, Ventures and Adventures of Willard Glazier (the Soldier-Author), in War and Literature. By John Algernon Owens." This book devotes its last nine chapters to the crowning work of Captain Glazier's life, the discovery of the source of the Mississippi River, holding him up to the youth of America as "an example which all men would do well to reflect upon and imitate."

Finally, having exhausted one continent, he sought other worlds to conquer, and sent his map, with a modest communication, to the Secretary of the Royal Geographical Society of England. The map and the captain's letter* were duly pub-

---

* The following is a copy of Captain Glazier's letter to the Royal Geographical Society, as published in the society's "Monthly Record" for January, 1885.

"DISCOVERY OF THE TRUE SOURCE OF THE MISSISSIPPI.

BY CAPTAIN WILLARD GLAZIER (U. S.).

"The true source of the Mississippi has been a vexed question among American geographers for some time, the country around its head-waters being in a very wild condition, inhabited only by Indians, and access to it difficult of accomplishment. In June, 1881, I organized and led an expedition with the object of settling forever the question of the source of our great river. We proceeded *via* Leech Lake to Lake Itasca, and, accompanied by an old Indian guide, pushed forward to the South, and were rewarded by the discovery of another lake of considerable size, which proves to be, without the shadow of a doubt, the true source of the Mississippi, in lat. 47' 13' 25". From notes taken during the ascent, it cannot be less than three feet above Lake Itasca—the hitherto supposed source of the river. The Mississippi may, therefore, be said to originate in an altitude 1,578 feet above the Atlantic Ocean. Its length, taking former data as the basis, may be placed at 3,184 miles.

lished in the "Monthly Record of Geography," issued under the authority of the Council of the Society, January, 1885, and, later, the thanks of the society were conveyed to Captain Glazier by order of the council, in an autograph letter from the secretary of that august body.

During the past year a friend of the captain, fortified by numerous scrap-books containing the record of the above indorsements and publications, has been industriously visiting publishers of geographical text-books and reference atlases, to secure at their hands the insertion of Lake Glazier on their maps, and a statement in the text to the effect that it is the head and source of the Mississippi. How generally this effort has been successful the forthcoming editions of such works will show. In a number of cases the change has already been made. A recent letter from this gentleman says:

"In answer to your question, I may state that Captain Glazier's claim to the discovery of the *true* source of the Mississippi is acknowledged by nearly every leading geographer in the country; there are now but very few exceptions.

"I have in my possession hundreds of clippings from almost every paper published on the banks of the Mississippi ; from Aitken and Brainerd, in the extreme north, to New Orleans, in the south. The St. Louis papers had many articles on the subject, and *all* recognized the *fact* of the discovery, and commented on the enterprise of the discoverer."

THE FACTS IN THE CASE.

Now, with this record already made up, it may be rash in me to dispute the validity of Captain Glazier's claim. He has filed a general *caveat*, and it has been very commonly conceded to make good his case. The letters-patent of greatness have already been issued to him, apparently from the highest authorities.

"The origin of the river in the remote and unfrequented region of country between Leech Lake and Red River, not less than an entire degree of latitude south of Turtle Lake, which was for many years regarded as the source, throws both forks of the stream out of the usual route of the fur trade, and furnishes, perhaps, the best reason why its head has remained so long enveloped in obscurity.

"I take the liberty of inclosing herewith a map showing my route and the true source of the Mississippi.

"To the SECRETARY, ROYAL GEOGRAPHICAL SOCIETY.

"MILWAUKEE, WISCONSIN, *June* 17, 1884."

However, to begin with, it may be well to state a few facts, most of which will be news to Captain Glazier:

First.—"Lake Glazier" is in reality Elk Lake, as laid down on the map of the United States General Land Office.*

Elk Lake lies mainly in Section 22 of Township No. 143 North, Range 36 West of the 5th Principal Meridian, the same being in the State of Minnesota. The lake lies south of the south-west arm of Lake Itasca, with which it is connected by a small stream about 400 feet long. An eighth of a mile to the west of this stream the distance between the marshy borders of Lake Itasca and Elk Lake is scarcely more than 100 feet.

Elk Lake is 1¼ miles long, ⅝ of a mile wide, and its circum-

---

* Regarding the identity of "Lake Glazier" and Elk Lake it is needless to argue. A comparison of the maps of Glazier and the Land Office Surveyors (see next page) will satisfy any one on this point. Glazier's description fits Elk Lake and no other in that whole region. The following description of the lake, by a member of Captain Glazier's own party, Mr. Bartlett Channing Paine, in a letter to the St. Paul "Pioneer-Press," dated August 8, 1881, applies to Elk Lake, and to that alone :

"We started for the upper end of the lake [Itasca] early next morning, finding, when we reached it that it terminated in bulrushes and what seemed to be a swamp. Our guide, however, took us through the rushes, and we found that a small but swift stream entered here, up which with difficulty we pushed our canoes. *This stream is about half a mile long*, and flows from one of the prettiest lakes we have seen on our trip. The shores are high rather than marshy, and covered with verdure; and the lake, which is nearly round, its regularity being broken by

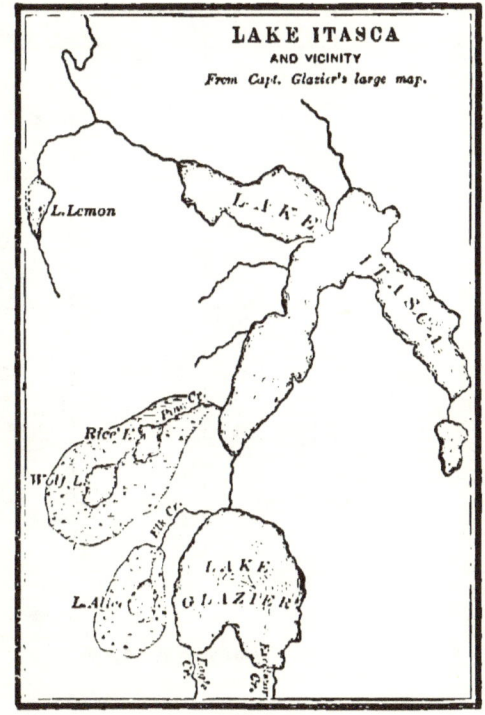

LAKE ITASCA
AND VICINITY
From Capt. Glazier's large map.

but one point, has a greatest diameter of a mile and a half, or perhaps two miles. Into this lake flow three small streams, which rise in marshy ground from a mile to three miles from the lake."

RANGE No. 36, WEST, 5th MERIDIAN.

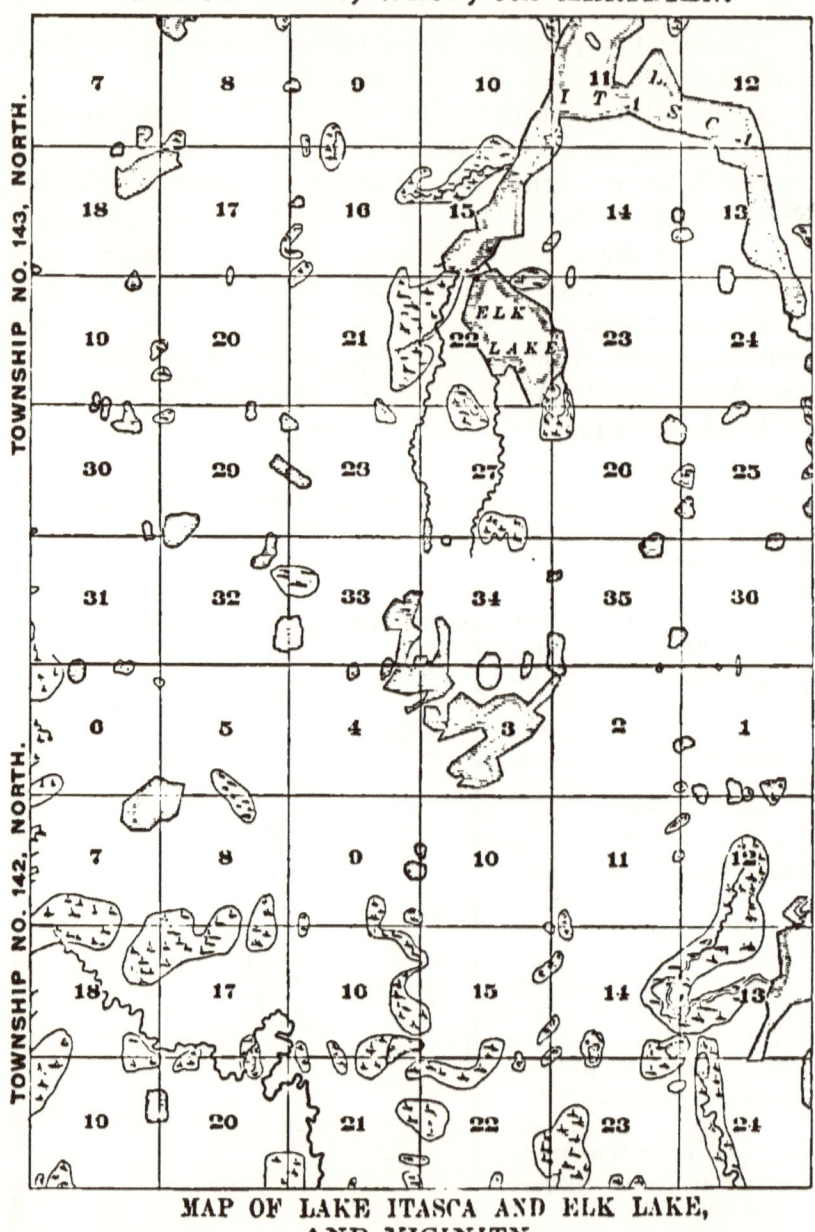

MAP OF LAKE ITASCA AND ELK LAKE,
AND VICINITY.

Reduced from fac-simile tracings of maps of the surveys made in October, 1875, and deposited in the
General Land Office at Washington, February, 1876. EDWIN S. HALL AND ASSISTANTS, SURVEYORS.

ference, as meandered by the government surveyors, is just 240 chains, or 3 miles.

Second.—Elk Lake was surveyed and definitely outlined by Surveyor Edwin S. Hall and his assistants, who spent two weeks in the survey of the township (36 square miles), from October 11 to October 25, 1875.

At four points, where the margin of the lake is intersected by the boundary-line of Section 22, Mr. Hall placed posts, numbered in their order 26, 27, 28, and 29; and these posts had been standing several years when Captain Glazier "discovered" the lake in 1881.

The map of the township was completed and certified as correct, February 3, 1876, by Surveyor-General J. H. Baker, of the St. Paul Land Office. It was by him transmitted to the General Land Office at Washington, where it was received February 19, 1876. Finally, it was officially verified and posted May 3, 1876, since which date it has been accessible as public property to any citizen of the United States who chose to ask for it. If Captain Glazier had sent *three dollars* to the Commissioner of the General Land Office he would have received a fac-simile tracing of this map, certified to be correct; and thus he might have discovered "Lake Glazier," and saved $9,997 of the $10,000 which his friends say he expended on this expedition, for the love of science and the glory of Captain Willard Glazier.

Third.—"The first white man who is known to have visited Lake Itasca was Wm. Morrison," an explorer and Indian trader, in the employ of the Hudson Bay Company, and afterward of Lord Selkirk, who ascended the main stream of the Mississippi and spent the winter of 1803–1804 in the vicinity of Lake Itasca, then called Elk Lake.*

---

* "Minnesota Geol. Survey—Final Report," vol. i., p. 26. The title of Morrison is based on letters from himself and his brother, Allan Morrison, first published in 1856. See "Minnesota Historical Collections," vol. i., p. 417, etc. The statements of the brothers Morrison have generally been received without question by scientists and geographers in Minnesota; and in his letter Allan Morrison expresses surprise that any one should be ignorant of the title of his brother to the discovery of Itasca prior to Schoolcraft. It is a curious fact, however, that Allan Morrison acted as guide for Charles Lanman for a number of weeks in 1846, during which time they visited Itasca Lake; and that Lanman, in his published account of the trip, nowhere mentions Wm. Morrison, or intimates that he was ever at the source of the Mississippi, but definitely ascribes the discovery to Schoolcraft in 1832. See Lanman's "Adventures in the Wilderness," vol. i., pages 48, 75, etc. I venture the opinion that Morrison

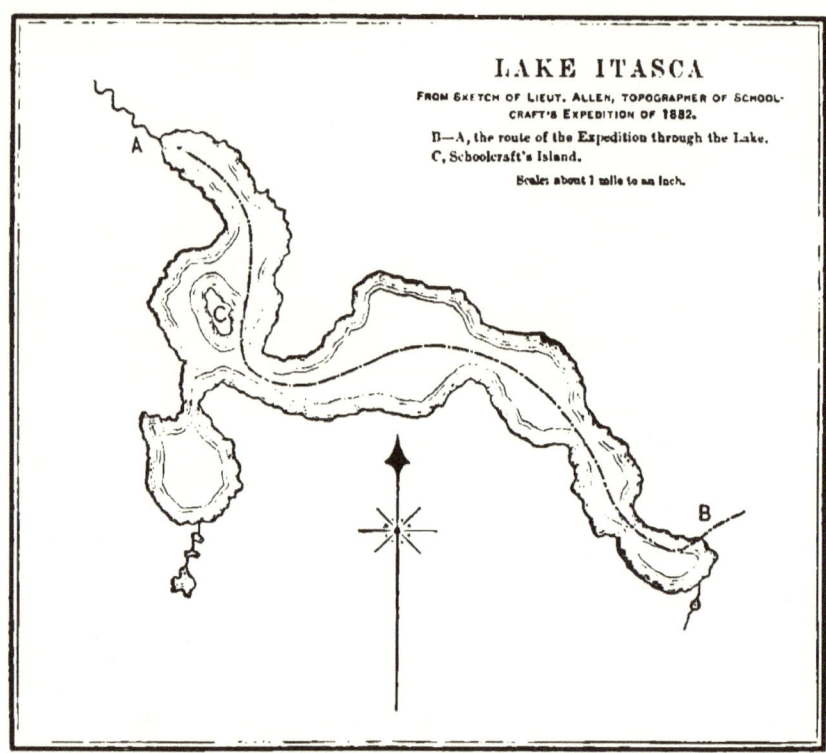

LAKE ITASCA

FROM SKETCH OF LIEUT. ALLEN, TOPOGRAPHER OF SCHOOL-
CRAFT'S EXPEDITION OF 1882.

B—A, the route of the Expedition through the Lake.
C, Schoolcraft's Island.

Scale: about 1 mile to an Inch.

Fourth.—Itasca Lake was visited in 1832 by Henry Rowe Schoolcraft and his party. They entered the lake at the head of the south-eastern arm, the afternoon of July 12, 1832, and left it early the next day by its outlet (the Mississippi River), at the extremity of the northern arm. They did not explore at all the south-western arm,* and so did not go near Elk Lake. But

first identified his Elk Lake of 1804 with Schoolcraft's Itasca when he read Schoolcraft's "Summary Narrative" (1855); and that it is safe to say that if Morrison discovered Lake Itasca, Schoolcraft discovered Morrison.

* There is no statement to this effect in Schoolcraft's report, but a comparison of Lieutenant Allen's map with that of the government surveyors must satisfy any one that the drawing of the south-western arm was made from the crude delineations of Indian guides. The south-eastern and northern parts of the lake are in remarkable accord with the actual surveys of 1875. The south-western arm is so very inaccurate in Lieutenant Allen's drawing that it is certain, if any of the party visited it, he must have been one of the guides sent merely to see if there was an inlet, and to report on its size, etc. This much, but not more, might be inferred from Schoolcraft's comparison of the volume of water discharged by the lake with that received through its inlet. See "Schoolcraft's Narrative," 1834, p. 58.

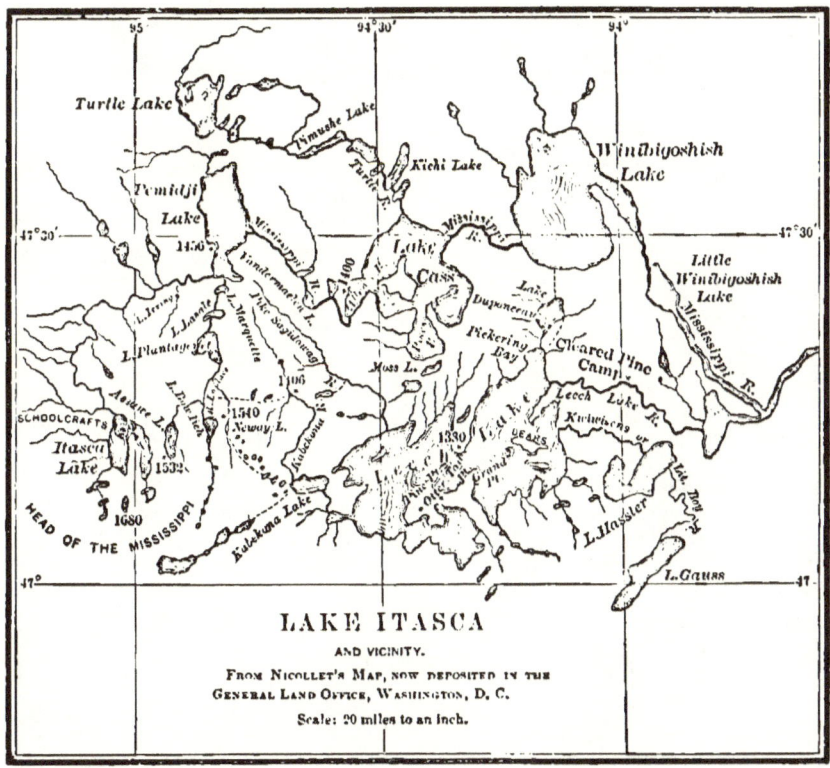

LAKE ITASCA

AND VICINITY.

From Nicollet's Map, now deposited in the
General Land Office, Washington, D. C.

Scale: 20 miles to an inch.

Lieutenant Allen, the topographer of the party, drew a map of Itasca Lake from his own observations and the reports of the Indian guides; and this map shows a south-western arm much shorter than the reality, but ending in a nearly circular extension, connected with the main lake by a narrow channel.

Fifth.—Mr. Jean N. Nicollet, a distinguished French scholar and explorer, in July, 1836, spent three days exploring the country to the south of the south-western arm of Lake Itasca. His map of the Upper Mississippi country, now deposited in the General Land Office, a copy of which was published by the government with his report, is on a very small scale, and does not show any lake corresponding to Elk Lake; but, fortunately, among Nicollet's notes and papers in the office of the Chief of Engineers of the United States Army, at Washington, there has been found a map of the sources of the Mississippi and Red River of the North, and this map is on a much larger scale, clearly showing Elk Lake in the very location where the gov-

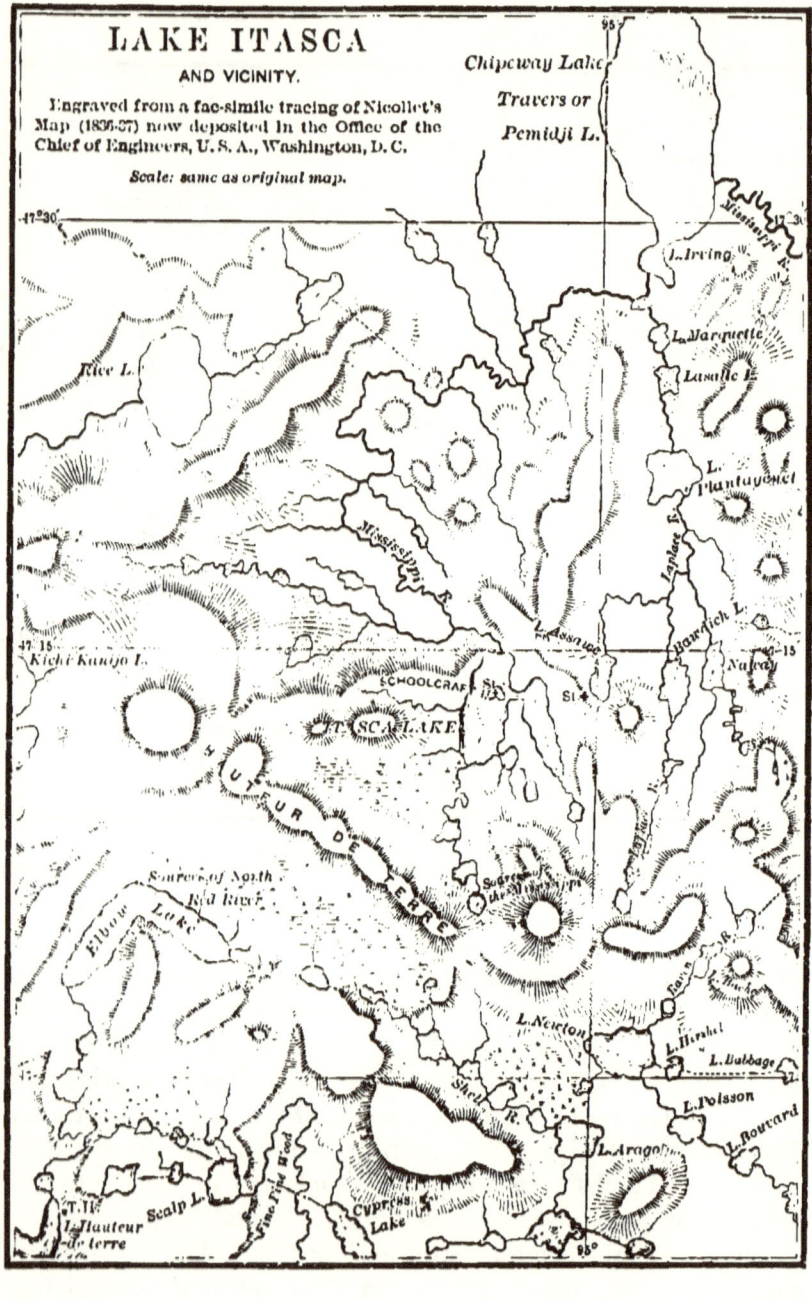

LAKE ITASCA

AND VICINITY.

Engraved from a fac-simile tracing of Nicollet's
Map (1836-37) now deposited in the Office of the
Chief of Engineers, U. S. A., Washington, D. C.

Scale: same as original map.

Chipeway Lake

Travers or
Pemidji L.

L. Irving

L. Marquette

Lasalle L.

Rice L.

Mississippi

L. Plantagenet

Hardich L.

Nakay

Kichi Kanijo L.

SCHOOLCRAF

L. SCALP LAKE

H T E U R D E

Sources of North
Red River

T E R R E

Elbow Lake

Sources
des M

L. Newton

L. Henkel

L. Bulbage

Shell R.

L. Poisson

L. Bouvard

L. Arago

Scalp L.

Cypress Lake

La Hauteur
de terre

ernment surveyors and Captain Glazier found it. There is no mistaking its identity. It is there, even to the three feeders which Captain Glazier found.* It is evident, however, that Nicollet regarded the lake as of minor importance, not giving it any separate name, but rather considering it an extension of the larger lake, Itasca.

Sixth.—In June, 1872, Mr. Julius Chambers, a staff correspondent of the "New York Herald," visited Lake Itasca and explored that lake and its borders. On June 10 he ascended one of the feeders of the south-western arm of the lake. After going a distance which he estimated at about a third of a mile he came to a small lake, a quarter of a mile in width, and, including a floating bog at its southern end, probably a mile or more in length. The land separating this lake from Lake Itasca he found to be a low tamarack swamp. If the map of the government surveyors is correct, this lake found by Mr. Chambers is no other than Elk Lake. His sketch† of the two lakes is certainly inaccurate in detail, but I think it will satisfy any one that he found the original of "Lake Glazier;" and it is just what it professes to be, the rough note-book drawing of a canoeist, made from memory after a day's hard paddling and tramping, when a hard way seemed a long way, and an easy pull measured a short distance.

Seventh.—In the year 1880 Mr. O. E. Garrison, of St. Cloud, Minn., visited the sources of the Mississippi, under joint instructions from the Superintendent of the Tenth Census of the United States and the Director of the Geological Survey of Minnesota. He proceeded from the south across the height of land, a route different from that of either Morrison, Schoolcraft, Nicollet, or Chambers. July 29 he encamped on the stream described by Nicollet as the real upper course of the Mississippi; July 30 he encamped on the south-western shore of Elk Lake; July 31 he sailed through Elk Lake and into Lake Itasca, and on that night

---

* A fac-simile engraving of a part of this larger map of Nicollet's is given herewith. I do not know that it has ever before been published, or that its existence among Nicollet's papers has been generally known.

† Some time after the most of this paper was in type I learned the name and address of the "Herald" correspondent of 1872. Mr. Chambers at once kindly placed his notes at my service, and a copy of his note-book map is here reproduced for the first time. See next page.

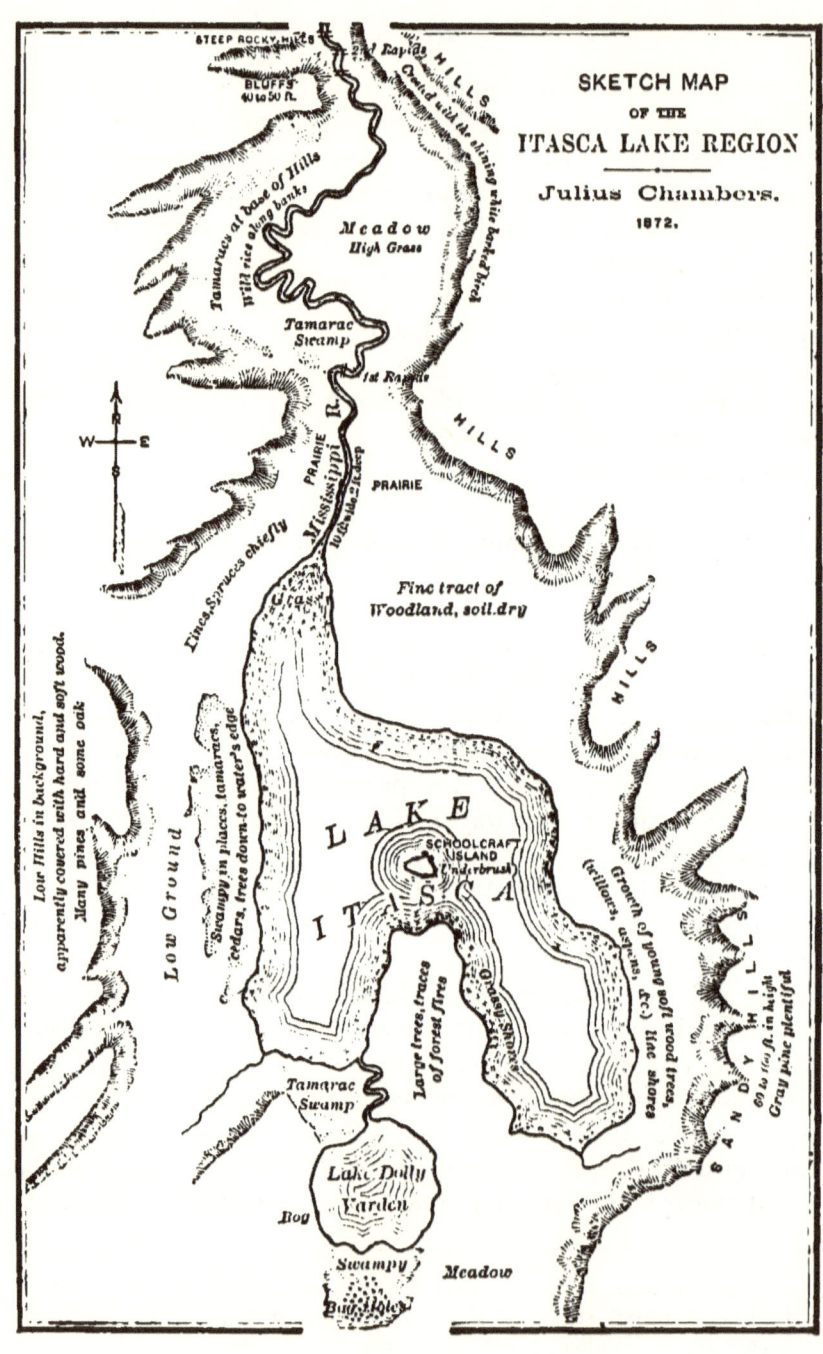

SKETCH MAP
OF THE
ITASCA LAKE REGION

Julius Chambers.

1872.

and the night succeeding he encamped on the west shore of Itasca. In all he spent about two weeks exploring the two townships, Nos. 142 and 143, N., R. 36; and this in July, 1880, a full year before Captain Glazier discovered his lake.

Eighth.—Mr. C. M. Terry, who made a close personal study of the water systems of Minnesota for the State Geological and Natural History Survey, in a paper on the Hydrology of Minnesota,[*] writes as follows:

"The inlets of the lake [Itasca] are on the shorter or south-west arm. There are five of them. They are small streams draining the swamps and springs in the vicinity. Less than a quarter of a mile south of the southwest arm is a little lake called Elk Lake. It has an area of about 200 acres. It is a mile long and half a mile wide. It is a tributary of Itasca Lake, through a small creek which connects them. Elk Lake has two or three small streams flowing into it from the south. The principal stream tributary to Itasca Lake, directly, also flows from the south, and is three or four miles in length. It is rather a refinement of exactness to call Elk Lake, *as some explorers have*, the ultimate source of the Mississippi. Itasca Lake has been in possession of the honor so long that its claim ought not to be disputed, and certainly it is sufficiently minute, remote, and sylvan to answer all the requirements of an ideal source."

So, a year before Glazier's expedition, Mr. Terry had already found "some explorers" who sought to dignify Elk Lake at the expense of Itasca. But there is no need of further enumeration of Glazier's predecessors. [†]

Ninth.—Elk Lake is the name originally applied to the whole of Lake Itasca. The Indians called it "*Omushkös*,[‡] which is the Chippewa name of the elk." "The Canadian French call this animal *la Biche*, from *Biche*, a hind," and the French-Indian guides in the service of the old fur companies called the lake *Lac la Biche*.[§] The name Itasca was coined by Mr. Schoolcraft for the occasion, from the Latin words *verITAS cAput*, the true source.

---

[*] "Ninth Annual Report of the Geological and Natural History Survey of Minnesota," 1880, p. 231.

[†] Among these predecessors might be named, Charles Lanman in 1846; Rev. Mr. Ayer and his son, Lyman Ayer (now residing at Little Falls, Minn.), in 1849; Mr. Wm. Bangs, of White Earth, Minn., in 1865; Mr. W. E. Neal, of Minneapolis, Minn., in 1880 and again in 1881; the Rev. J. B. Gilfillan, of White Earth, Minn., in May, 1881; and a number of others.

[‡] "Schoolcraft's Summary Narrative," Philadelphia, 1855, p. 243.

[§] "Schoolcraft's Summary Narrative," Philadelphia, 1855, p. 132.

THE NATURE OF THE ITASCAN REGION.

From the above facts the natural inference is that Mr. Schoolcraft, Lieutenant Allen, Mr. Nicollet, and the Indian guides and *voyageurs* of their day found Elk Lake and Lake

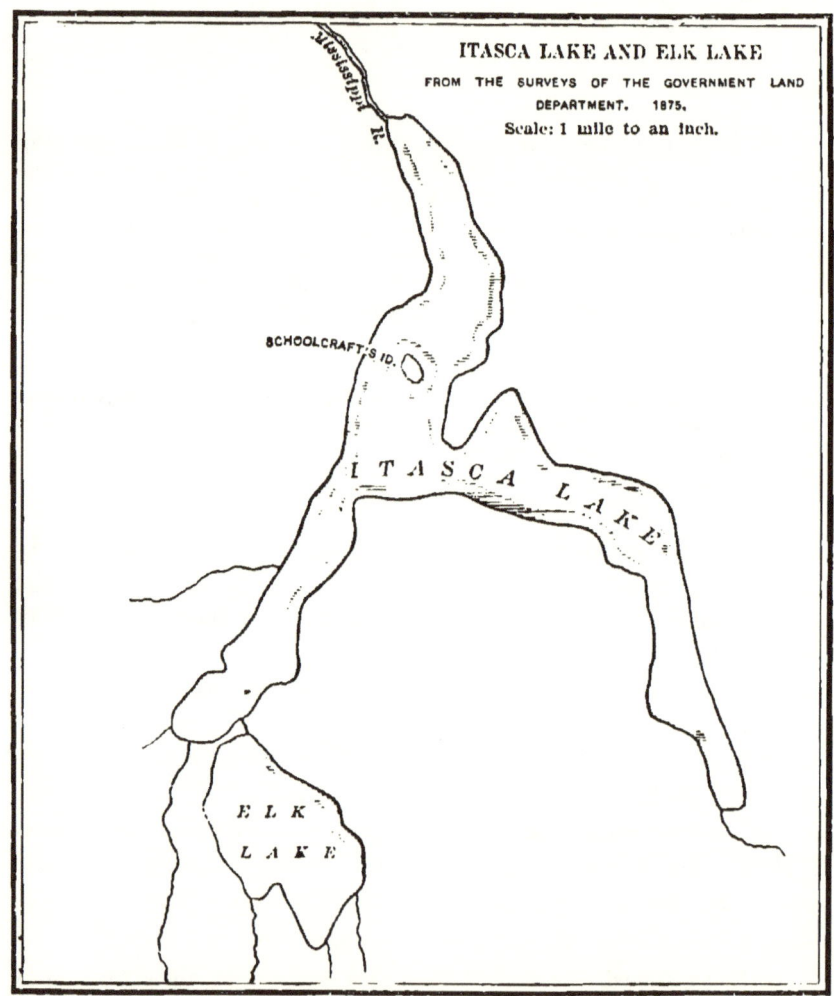

ITASCA LAKE AND ELK LAKE

FROM THE SURVEYS OF THE GOVERNMENT LAND DEPARTMENT. 1875.

Scale: 1 mile to an inch.

Itasca to be closely connected bodies of water, and that the minor lake still retains the name of Elk Lake by reason of its having been at one time practically continuous with Lake Itasca.

Further, all travelers in this region report a large number of lakes and ponds without any visible outlet, and streams and lakes that Nicollet reported as existing in 1836, either do not appear on the government maps, or their proportions are much reduced and they have ceased to be connected with each other. After making all necessary allowance for the fact that the Government Land-Office maps do not assume to follow up minor streams, and do not give the outlines or dimensions of lakes which are not intersected by the boundary-lines of sections, it still remains probable that there has been a considerable decrease in the amount of natural water supply during the past fifty years, and a consequent subsidence of the water-level in many of the lakes on the higher slopes of the heights of land in Minnesota. This would naturally affect first the springs and ponds that feed the lakes, and finally the lakes themselves, which form the first reservoirs of the waters of the Mississippi. On the other hand, the growth of any natural obstruction across the outlet of a marshy pond or spring would have the effect of spreading it out into a broad, shallow lakelet. Mr. Garrison, in his report to the State Geologist, speaks of coming upon the beds of dried-up ponds and streams, and also of finding no outlet to lakes that had evidently been formerly drained. The lakes in Secs. 33 and 34, Tp. 143, and in Secs. 3 and 4, Tp. 142, which he says were "marked on the old maps as having an outlet to the north and being therefore the ultimate sources of the Mississippi," were carefully explored by him, and no outlet was found in any direction. If these two lakes ever belonged to the Itasca basin, and had a free outlet to the northward, they were much smaller than they now appear, while the lake below, on the stream shown in the N. W. quarter of Sec. 34, Tp. 143, was correspondingly larger. But this latter pond, when Mr. Garrison saw it, was the head of the "largest feeder to Lake Itasca, worthy to be considered as the utmost source of the Mississippi." * Thus many changes have evidently occurred in this region, and probably some very important ones, within the past fifty years, since Nicollet's explorations in 1836.

Mr. Chambers did not make any careful observations with reference to this question, but he informs me that there are many

---

* "There are several streams entering the lake [Itasca] which have disputed the right to be the extreme source. The one adopted by Nicollet and by me in the preceding narrative is the largest feeder of the lake, and should have the name."—O. E. Garrison, in "Ninth Annual Report of the State Geological Survey of Minnesota," for the year 1880, pp. 219, 220.

places where a week of rainy weather would change entirely the outline of many of the lakes throughout this region, and that Elk and Itasca lakes may easily have been one continuous body of water years ago.

This digression simply proves that there is in reality an unsolved problem regarding the head-waters of the Mississippi and Lake Itasca. The manifest discrepancies between the accounts and maps of Schoolcraft (Lieut. Allen), Nicollet, and the government surveyors show this; but Captain Glazier lost sight of it entirely. Had he been a genuine devotee of science, had he ever made anything like a careful study of the problem he was undertaking to solve, he would have informed himself as to the real state of knowledge on the subject before starting out on his fool's errand to the wilds of Minnesota.

Captain Glazier's information in regard to Mississippi exploration seems to have begun and ended with what he could glean from Schoolcraft's narratives of his various expeditions of fifty years before. How well he studied them and how freely he made use of them I may be able to show farther on in this paper.

MORE FACTS.

In passing, it may be well to state two other matters of fact for the information of Captain Glazier, to wit:

Tenth.—Mr. Chambers made the trip of the entire length of the Mississippi River, from the sources of Elk Lake to the Gulf of Mexico, at the South-west Pass, going as far as Quincy, Ill., in his canoe, and the rest of the way by steamer, but every mile of the way by water.

Eleventh.—(And this will tax Captain Glazier's credulity most of all) Mr. Chambers did not make any stump speech; did not rate himself a great discoverer; made no appeal to the Geographical Societies of the world; did not call his lake, Lake Chambers, but simple Dolly Varden (after the name of his canoe); made no addresses; was greeted by no brass bands; and did not finally receive the freedom of the city of New Orleans or the honors of its Academy of Sciences; but his letters are to be found in the "Herald" of June 20, 27, July 2, 6, 9, 13, 22, and 27, 1872, the one in the issue of July 6 being devoted to the exploration of Elk Lake.

JEAN NICOLAS NICOLLET.

But it is of the first importance to any one pretending to a knowledge of the Upper Mississippi, to know something of Mr. J. N. Nicollet, who devoted the last and best years of his life to the exploration of the hydrographic basin of that river.

Jean Nicolas Nicollet was born at Cluses, France, in July, 1786. A favorite pupil of the great Laplace, he early distinguished himself as an original observer and student. His works, published in France before he came to this country, were of high merit. In 1832 he came to the United States for the purpose, as he tells us, "of making a scientific tour and with the view of contributing to the progressive increase of knowledge in the physical geography of North America." His first tour was to the western affluents of the Mississippi, whose head-waters he explored. Thence he proceeded to the Upper Mississippi, and there decided to visit the source of that river. Mr. Nicollet reached Lake Itasca late in August, 1836, and spent three days in thoroughly exploring the country for miles around. His account of this trip is embodied in a report to Colonel J. J. Abert, Chief of the Corps of Topographical Engineers of the Army, made after a second visit to the Upper Mississippi. Mr. Nicollet had returned to the East somewhat broken in health, and was resting with friends in Baltimore, when, in April, 1838, he received the invitation from the War Department to conduct an expedition for the fuller survey of the Mississippi Valley. He accordingly returned and spent a part of two years following in the same region.

In the 2d Session of the 26th Congress, the Senate ordered the map and report of Mr. Nicollet completed and printed. The failing health of the explorer made this work slow and arduous, and it was still incomplete when he died, September 11, 1843. A note appended to his report, bearing date September 13, 1843, says:

"Thus far Mr. Nicollet had written when death put an end to his labors, and before he had been able to revise his report, which had been returned to him for that purpose, and also to add the astronomical observations upon which his calculations were founded. These observations form parts of his journals, which are to be deposited in the Bureau of the Corps of Topographical Engineers."

It is to be regretted that Mr. Nicollet did not live to finish and correct his report, but the report, as he left it, was duly published as Executive Document No. 237 of the 2d Session, 26th Congress, and copies are undoubtedly to be found in many of the public libraries of the country.*

With these preliminary observations I now propose to quote from Mr. Nicollet's report such parts as relate to his trip to the source of the Mississippi. I begin these quotations at the point where he decides to leave the Mississippi at Crow Wing River† and go across the country to Leech Lake on his way to Itasca.

AT ELK LAKE IN 1836.

" On my arrival at the Crow Wing River, I could not but reflect that the Mississippi before me had been thoroughly explored during the expeditions of Major Pike, General Cass, and Mr. Schoolcraft, whose accounts were very generally known to the public. I thought, therefore, that it might be advisable to attempt another route across the country ; so that, leaving the Crow Wing at the distance of three miles from its mouth, I ascended the Gayashk, or Gull River, and the pretty lake having the same name. Thence I proceeded as far as Pine River, taking occasion to visit Kadikomeg, or White Fish Lake ; then, again ascending the east fork of Pine River, I reached the Kwiwisens, or Little Boy River, which I descended through a succession of lakes, and over small rapids, as far as Leech Lake. I spent a week on the borders of this beautiful sheet of water, my tent being most generally pitched on Otter Tail Point. This was the residence of my principal guide, Francis Brunet, a man six feet three inches high—a giant of great strength, but, at the same time, full of the milk of human kindness, and withal, an excellent natural geographer. . . .

" Having lessened my equipage, and made arrangements to proceed to the source of the Mississippi, I left Leech Lake in a bark canoe of sufficient size to contain my instruments, some provisions, and three persons besides myself, who were Desire, Francis Brunet, and a respectable Chippewa named Kegwed-

---

* " Report intended to Illustrate a Map of the Hydrographic Basin of the Upper Mississippi River, made by J. N. Nicollet, while in employ under the Bureau of the Corps of Topographical Engineers." Washington: Blair & Rives, Printers. 1843. This report and the accompanying map were also published by order of the House of Representatives, in the 2d Session of the 28th Congress, appearing as Executive Document No. 52. As indicating the lack of proof-reading, I notice that in the report Mr. Nicollet's name is always printed J. N. Nicollet.

† Crow Wing River is but a few miles below Brainerd, where Captain Glazier also left the Mississippi for Leech Lake, and both explorers followed nearly the same trail from Leech Lake to Lake Itasca. However, I do not see in this or in Captain Glazier's account anything which would lead me to suppose that he had read Nicollet's report before starting upon his trip. In fact, the absence of direct appropriation of Nicollet's language leads to the conclusion that Captain Glazier wrote in entire ignorance of his predecessor's work.

zissag, who was well acquainted with the country I wished to visit, and which he called his own, as he was in the habit of hunting over it.

"Leaving Leech Lake, we crossed several small lakes, and reached the one called Kabekonang, the name being derived from *kabe*, to disembark, and *mikan*, a path or trail, or, in its full meaning, ' the place where one disembarks to take up the trail or route.' We ascended the river which bears the same name, and, flowing in a narrow and deep valley, is said not to freeze before January, nor, when frozen, to thaw until July. . . .

"From the sources of Kabekonang (sometimes shortly called Kabekona) we made a portage of five miles, that brought us to the River La Place, which we ascended as far as one mile south of Assawa Lake, where we found a circular camp used four years previously by Mr. Schoolcraft. But here we were assailed by swarms of mosquitoes, that came pouring upon us in torrents; so as, at three different times, to extinguish the lights of my lanterns, whilst I was making my astronomical observations.

"The next morning we were up at half-past four, preparing for a portage of about six miles, which was before us, and was to bring us to Itasca Lake, the principal basin on the head-waters of the Mississippi, as well as the projected terminus of my excursion. . . .

" I shall not dwell further on the description of this portage, the first three miles of which, including a momentary rest afforded by the crossing of a small lake, were attended with so many difficulties that it took me five hours to achieve that which my men went over in three ; the last three miles being over a succession of ascents and descents, between which were most commonly sloughs. The soil is sandy and gravelly, overspread with erratic blocks ; but there is a great variety of evergreens, and they are larger than in the region previously mentioned. I measured the elevation of the most prominent ridges. The last in the series, being also the highest, is 120 feet above the waters of Lake Itasca. This ridge, with a rapid descent, led us to the borders of the lake, where I took a barometrical observation at noon.

"My next move was to pitch my tent on Schoolcraft's Island. The staff, at the top of which that gentleman informed us he had raised the American flag, had been cut down by the Indians. I made use of what remained of it to fix upon it my artificial horizon, and immediately proceeded to make astronomical observations, and take up the exploration of the sources of the Mississippi.

"The Mississippi holds its own from its very origin; for it is not necessary to suppose, as has been done, that Lake Itasca may be supplied with invisible sources, to justify the character of a remarkable stream, which it assumes at its issue from this lake. There are five creeks that fall into it, formed by innumerable streamlets oozing from the clay-beds at the bases of the hills, that consist of an accumulation of sand, gravel, and clay, intermixed with erratic fragments ; being a more prominent portion of the erratic deposits previously described, and which here is known by the name of 'Hauteurs des Terres'—heights of land. . . .

" The waters supplied by the north flank of these heights of land—still on the south side of Lake Itasca—give origin to the five creeks of which I have spoken above. These are the waters which I consider to be the utmost sources of the Mississippi. . . .

" Now, of the five creeks that empty into Itasca Lake, one empties into the east bay of the lake ; the four others into the west bay. I visited the whole of them ; and among the latter there is one remarkable above the others, inasmuch as its course is longer, and its waters more abundant : so that, in obedience to the geographical rule, 'that the sources of a river are those that are most distant from its mouth,' this creek is truly the infant Mississippi; all others below, its feeders and tributaries.   The day on which I explored this principal creek (August 29, 1836), I judged that, at its entrance into Itasca Lake, its bed was from fifteen to twenty feet wide, and the depth of water from two to three feet.   We stemmed its pretty brisk current during ten or twenty minutes ; but the obstructions occasioned by the fall of trees compelled us to abandon the canoe and to seek its springs on foot, along the hills.   After a walk of three miles, during which we took care not to lose sight of the Mississippi, my guides informed me that it was better to descend into the trough of the valley ; when, accordingly, we found numberless streamlets oozing from the bases of the hills. . . .

  " As a further description of these head-waters, I may add that they unite at a small distance from the hills whence they originate, and form a small lake, from whence the Mississippi flows with a breadth of a foot and a half, and a depth of one foot.   At no great distance, however, this rivulet, uniting itself with other streamlets coming from other directions, supplies a second minor lake. . . .

  " From this lake issues a rivulet, necessarily of increased importance—a cradled Hercules, giving promise of the strength of his maturity ; for its velocity has increased ; it transports the smaller branches of trees ; it begins to form sand-bars; its bends are more decided, until it subsides again into the basin of a third lake somewhat larger than the two preceding.   Having here acquired new vigor, and tried its consequence upon an additional length of two or three miles, it finally empties into Itasca Lake, which is the principal reservoir of all the sources to which it owes all its subsequent majesty. . . .

  " The honor of having first explored the sources of the Mississippi, and introduced a knowledge of them into physical geography, belongs to Mr. Schoolcraft and Lieutenant Allen.   I come only after these gentlemen ; but I may be permitted to claim some merit for having completed what was wanting for a full geographical account of these sources.   Moreover, I am, I believe, the first traveler, who has carried with him astronomical instruments, and put them to profitable account along the whole course of the Mississippi, from its mouth to its sources. . . .

  " After having devoted three days to an exploration of the sources of the Mississippi, and spent portions of the night in making astronomical observations, I took leave of Itasca Lake, to the examination of which the expedition that preceded me by four years had devoted but a short time."

SCHOOLCRAFT AND NICOLLET.

Such is the simple, modest account of a true scientist, a genuine explorer.   How refreshing it reads after the noisy self-advertising of the modern charlatan !   Certainly this expedition of Nicollet's should not have been unknown to a man who had been studying the problem of the Mississippi for years, and was willing to give his life to the solution of its mystery. But Captain Glazier seems never to have read anything more recent than Mr. Schoolcraft's narrative of the expedition of 1832, for he regards him as the last of his predecessors at Lake Itasca. Here is the way he commiserates Schoolcraft on his failure. I quote from "Sword and Pen," pages 472, 473:

"Much astonishment was expressed by those of the party who were aware of Schoolcraft's expedition of 1832, that he should have missed finding this lake, so closely connected with Itasca, and various were the surmises as to the cause of this remarkable oversight. . . . By far the most probable theory, however, was advanced by Captain Glazier, who stated, quoting Schoolcraft himself as authority, that when he reached Itasca he was too much hurried to make a thorough exploration. He had an engagement to meet some Indians in council at the mouth of the Crow Wing River, fully seven days' journey from this point, and he did not have more than seven days to do it in. . . . He never saw the beautiful lake to the south of Itasca, fed by the springs and streams of the marshes which gave birth to the infant Mississippi.

"Therefore he could not know that Itasca was but an expansion of the stream, like other lakes, in its onward course, a sudden growth, as it were, which gave promise of the vast proportions the mighty giant would hereafter assume. There would be something almost sad in his coming so near and yet missing the mark at which he had aimed, if it were not that he lived and *died* in the belief that he was right in the assertion that the Father of Waters rose in the lake which he, oddly enough, named Itasca."

Not too fast, Captain Glazier. Mr. Schoolcraft was not a mere superficial adventurer; and he lived down to the year of grace 1864. So it is safe to say he knew all about Mr. Nicollet and the remoter sources of the Mississippi, far more, indeed, than did Captain Glazier, even after his wonderful exploring expedition. This would go without proof, but the proof is easily to be had. If Captain Glazier will refer to Mr. Schoolcraft's "Summary Narrative" of his two expeditions to the head-waters of the Mississippi,* he will find evidence of this in abundance. He will find reference to Mr. Nicollet in the text and in foot-notes on pages viii., ix., 128, 133, 139, 142, 154, 244, 267, and 328. Furthermore, on pages 582–586, Mr. Schoolcraft gives in full the *Table of Geographical Positions on the Mississippi River, observed in 1836, by J. N. Nicollet.* The last item in this table gives the distance

---

* "Summary Narrative of an Exploratory Expedition to the Source of the Mississippi River, in 1820: Revised and Completed by the Discovery of its Origin in Itasca Lake, in 1832." By Henry R. Schoolcraft. Philadelphia: Lippincott, Grambo & Co. 1855.

from Schoolcraft's Island, in Itasca Lake, to the "*utmost sources of the Mississippi*, at the summit of the Hauteurs de Terre, or dividing-ridge between the Mississippi and the Red River of the North," as six miles, and the elevation of these sources as five feet above Lake Itasca. Mr. Schoolcraft's reference to Mr. Nicollet shows the most unquestioning confidence in the correctness and value of his discoveries. There was no thought of jealousy or depreciation; just as on the part of Mr. Nicollet there was no thought of claiming any credit above Mr. Schoolcraft and Lieutenant Allen. He was willing "to come after these gentlemen," and to be "permitted to claim some merit for having completed what was wanting for a full geographical account of these sources."

And this is exactly the relation between the explorer of 1832 and the one of 1836. The latter simply completed what was wanting of the work of Schoolcraft and his able assistant and topographer, Lieutenant Allen. They had not explored the remotest springs and ponds that fed Lake Itasca, but there is no doubt of their having a fairly accurate understanding of the location of these remoter sources of the river, from the reports of their Indian guides. For proof of this I refer to the map of Lake Itasca,[*] drawn by Lieutenant Allen, in part evidently from data furnished by the Indians, which shows a southern feeder running through a chain of small ponds. The stream appears shorter and the ponds smaller than Mr. Nicollet afterward found them to be, but the map proves that Schoolcraft was not such an extreme object of commiseration as Captain Glazier would have us think.

GUYOT AND NICOLLET.

Nor had the world entirely forgotten the facts in regard to this matter even before Captain Glazier made his "great discovery." The following passage, from Guyot's [†] "Introduction

---

[*] See "Schoolcraft's Summary Narrative," 1855, p. 243.

[†] There is especial satisfaction in coupling the names of Nicollet and Guyot in this connection. Nicollet was among the first of that considerable number of distinguished foreigners, not Englishmen, who in the maturity of their powers have come to this country, and devoted their lives and fortunes to the prosecution of scientific studies in the broad field furnished by the New World. Humboldt had, perhaps, given the grand impulse in this direction, though he returned to Europe at the end of his researches, and his especial field was

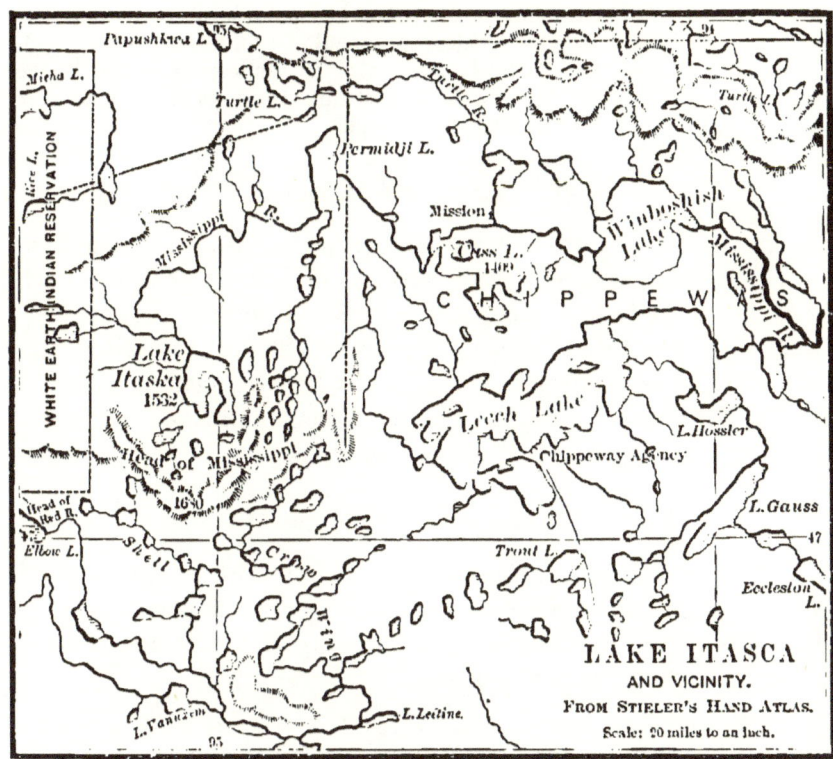

LAKE ITASCA
AND VICINITY.
FROM STIELER'S HAND ATLAS.
Scale: 20 miles to an inch.

to Geography," pages 12 and 13, was written in 1866, twenty years ago:

"We find, away in a forest of pine-woods, almost to the north border of our country, a great number of little springs. The hills from which these springs flow are not high, steep, and rocky, like those we found among the Appalachian Mountains, but they are low and rounded, and made of sand and clay. The little streams flow from the springs in these hills into a hollow, where they make a very small *pond* or *lake*. This little pond is the place where the great *Mississippi* begins its journey to the ocean. It is therefore called the *source* of the Mississippi. From this, the cradle of the Mississippi, flows a little brook so small you could easily leap across it, and not deep enough to prevent your wading through it.

"After the little brook has gone a distance of six* miles, it finds another

South America. But Nicollet deserves to stand with Humboldt, Guyot, and Agassiz in the first rank of scholars and investigators. Such men are certainly entitled to all the honors which they have won in the cause of science.

* This is an error of reckoning made by Guyot in common with other geographers. Nicollet places the utmost sources of the river about *six miles from Schoolcraft's Island,* in Lake Itasca, thus making their distance from Itasca Lake three or four miles

small, basin-shaped hollow, into which it flows. Four other little streams flow into the same basin, and their waters spread out and fill it, and form a small and beautiful lake. This is called *Itasca* Lake. It is always considered as the source of the Mississippi, because the little stream that flows into it is so very small that people do not call it the Mississippi."

PETERMANN AND NICOLLET.

As a still further and valuable evidence that the scientific world in general knew of the results of Nicollet's explorations, it is worth while to reproduce (see p. 33), from the highest German authority a small map of the sources of the Mississippi. It is a copy on an enlarged scale of a section of a map to be found in Dr. Petermann's "Stieler's Hand Atlas," published by Justus Perthes, of the Gotha Institute of Geography.

GLAZIER AND NICOLLET.

Captain Glazier himself seems to have had a vague idea of such an explorer as Nicollet, but in every case he places him before Schoolcraft in order of mention, and earlier in point of time. This is the way he speaks of him:

" Within the last century several expeditions have attempted to find the primal reservoir of the great river ; Beltrami, Nicollet, and Schoolcraft have *each in turn* claimed the goal of their explorations. . . . Schoolcraft *finally* located a lake which he named Itasca, as the fountain-head, in 1832, and succeeded in securing for it the recognition of geographers and map-makers." *

And again the captain shows his ignorance of Nicollet after this fashion:

"To stand at the source ; to look upon the remotest rills and springs which contribute to the birth of the great river of North America ; to write *finis* in the volume opened by the renowned De Soto more than three hundred years ago, and in which Marquette, La Salle, Hennepin, Joliet, Beltrami, Nicollet, and Schoolcraft *have successively* inscribed their names, was quite enough to revive the drooping spirits of the most depressed." †

All this seems very strange in the man who claims to be the last and not the least of the great line of heroes of Mississippi exploration. But I am not inclined to charge this perversion and suppression of history to anything worse than ignorance.

---

* "Am. Meteorological Journal," 1884, p. 176.
† "Am. Meteorological Journal," 1884, p. 322.

GLAZIER AND CHAMBERS.

While Captain Glazier should certainly have known very definitely of Mr. Nicollet's explorations in the region of Lake Itasca before he himself ventured into that field as an explorer, it is, however, not so surprising that he had not heard of the trip of the "Herald's" canoeist correspondent when he himself started for the North. But for the past two years there has been no excuse for his maintaining the claim that no one had been to Elk Lake before him and his party. If he knew nothing of Nicollet's explorations in 1836 and nothing of Surveyor Hall's work in 1875, he must at least have read, in the very paper that published his letter to Judge Daly, the following editorial reference to his predecessor of 1872:

" Unfortunately for him [Captain Glazier], however, this little lake seems to be the very body of water found twelve years ago by a special correspondent sent out by the ' Herald' to find the Mississippi's head-waters. In our paper of July 6, 1872, we published a letter in which our explorer reported that after forcing his canoe through a narrow, tortuous stream entering the south-western extremity of Lake Itasca, he suddenly entered a lake almost circular in outline, to which he gave the name of Dolly Varden."

CHAMBERS AT "LAKE GLAZIER" IN 1872.

Yet, lest he may not have taken the trouble to search the columns of the paper, I will reproduce the following from the letter as it originally appeared:

" The Dolly Varden was rid of every ounce of extra luggage, all being left with the guide and Indian at the camp near the outlet of Itasca, for the crew was about to start on a voyage in which he might have to carry her on his head. Everything in readiness, a small bag of hard bread and cold bacon and roast duck on board, the crew pushed out alone on the lake for a thorough circumnavigation of the shore. Under paddle the canoe coasted down the eastern side to reach the south-east end of the lake. The soundings to the first landing-place at an average of 300 feet from shore were 19, 15, 8, and 14 feet. Near the southern point a small stream enters the lake, but does not extend further than 1,500 feet back along the ridge between the edge of a meadow and a hill of pines. Here it is a tiny rivulet which trickles down from the rocks. The crew is satisfied that it does not flow throughout the year, and that it owes even its present size to the recent storms. . . .

" The crew then returned to the canoe and crossed to Schoolcraft Island, finding twelve feet of water about midway. It was not thought best to make a landing at this point, but the shore was followed on the side toward the mainland. The channel which separates the island is not more than 800 feet in width at the broadest point. The island bears the same general direction as the lake, its extremities being located north-west and south-east. . . .

"Crossing to the tamarack forest, which bounds the lake on the southern side, it was found to be quite swampy in places. Although frequent landings were made the cruise continued until, at the south-western angle of the lake, a small inlet was seen, from which issued a stream of clear water. It had cut for itself a channel, about four feet in depth and scarcely more in width, through the thick turf, and defied discoloration by its shiny banks. The heart of the crew beat in wild and hopeful expectancy. The Dolly was pushed up through this channel, and after about one-third of a mile of pushing, paddling, and hauling, the stream brought the craft to a small, round lake.

"The inlet had not been easy of navigation by any means, and growing much shallower after the first 150 feet, several portages had been made by dragging the boat across the sticks and logs in the tamarack swamp. The lake was not more than from 1,000 to 1,200 feet in diameter, and apparently about circular in shape. It was quite shallow, with considerable grass in places. The crew crossed to the opposite side, and found it a floating bog, a large lake, in fact, with a sod floating at one side, thus narrowing it down to the circular lakelet which had at first appeared. Beyond this bog, after a long tramp through water to the knees, no other streams or open lakes could be found. The same was found to be true after the lake was completely circumnavigated.

"Here then is the source of the largest river in the world ; here, in Cass County (now Hubbard County), Minnesota, in a small lake, scarcely one quarter of a mile in diameter,* in the midst of a floating bog, are the fountains which give birth to the Mississippi. The greatest depth of the lake was found to be only twelve feet. After bathing in the lake, for a small sandy beach exists near the outlet, the crew christened the little sheet of water Dolly Varden Lake, and he is resolved to maintain that name against all competitors."

Returning to Lake Itasca, Mr. Chambers started down the Mississippi in his canoe, and after traveling as far as Quincy, Illinois, by that craft, took steamer to St. Louis. Thence, also by steamer, he went to New Orleans and the Gulf of Mexico, which he entered by the South-west Pass, thus traversing the entire length of the river from its sources to its discharge into the Gulf some nine years before Captain Glazier performed the same exploit. But Mr. Chambers did not consider this achievement anything more than the vacation outing of a fagged journalist, and was probably satisfied if the proceeds of his letters paid the expenses of his trip.

GLAZIER AS AN EXPLORER.

I have noted the careful and painstaking way in which Nicollet pursued his investigations, devoting his days to explorations

---

* This is the estimated width of the lake. The length, including the floating bog which Mr. Chambers describes, is about a mile.

and much of his nights to astronomical observations. In contrast with this it is worth while to call attention to the superficial, drowsy way in which our modern explorer did his work. To do him full justice I give in his own words Captain Glazier's account of his movements from the time that he sighted Lake Itasca, "between three and four o'clock in the afternoon" of July 21, until he and his party quit Schoolcraft's Island and started down the river "at three o'clock in the afternoon" of July 22 : *

"On turning out of a thicket at the foot of the last elevation, between three and four o'clock in the afternoon, our longing eyes rested upon the waters of Lake Itasca. A few moments later we were floating on its placid bosom, and after a pull of between two and three miles reached Schoolcraft's Island. This island derives its name from Henry Rowe Schoolcraft, who discovered Itasca in 1832, and located it as the source of the Mississippi.

"Hitherto the claim of Schoolcraft has been unquestioned, and for half a century Lake Itasca has enjoyed the honor of standing at the head of the Father of Waters. . . .

"The exhausting portages of July 21st, between the east and west forks of the Mississippi, prepared us for a sleep which even the Minnesota mosquitoes could not disturb, and which was not broken until *long after the sun was glinting upon us through the trees on the morning of the twenty-second.* Although I had cautioned the guides to awaken me at dawn, I found them snoring lustily at six o'clock.

"As soon as all were astir Che-no-wa-ge-sic and the Lagards prepared breakfast. George struck tents and rolled the blankets, while Paine busied himself with an article for the St. Paul 'Pioneer-Press,' descriptive of our voyage to Lake Itasca. But little ceremony was observed at breakfast, which was served with a due regard to our scant rations, and consisted of a small slice of bacon and a 'flap-jack,' each of very meager dimensions. . . .

"Fully convinced that the statements of Che-no-wa-ge-sic were entirely trustworthy, and knowing from past experience that he was perfectly reliable as a guide, *we put our canoes into the water at eight o'clock,* and at once began coasting Itasca for its feeders. We found the outlets of six small streams, two having well-defined mouths, and four filtering into the lake through bogs.

"The upper end of the south-western arm is heavily margined with rushes and swamp grass, and it was not without considerable difficulty that we forced our way through this barrier into the larger of the two open streams which flow into this end of the lake.

"Although perfectly familiar with the topography of the country, and entirely confident that he could lead us to the beautiful lake which he had so often described, Che-no-wa-ge-sic was for some moments greatly disturbed by the network of rushes in which we found ourselves temporarily entangled. Leaping from his canoe, he pushed the rushes right and left with his paddle,

---

* This description is to be found in the "Am. Met. Journal," 1884, pages 262, 322, 324, 325, 327.

and soon, to our great delight, threw up his hands and gave a characteristic 'Chippewa yell,' thereby signifying that he had found the object of his search. Returning, he seized the bow of my canoe, and pulled it after him through the rushes out into the clear, glistening waters of the infant Mississippi, which at the point of entering Itasca is seven feet wide and about one foot deep.

" Slow and sinuous progress of two hundred yards brought us to a blockade of logs and shallow water. Determined to float in my canoe upon the surface of the lake towards which we were paddling, I directed the guides to remove the obstructions, and continued to urge the canoes rapidly forward, although opposed by a strong and constantly increasing current. Sometimes we found it necessary to lift the canoes over logs, and occasionally to remove diminutive, sand-bars from the bed of the stream with our paddles. As we neared the head of this primal section of the mighty river we could readily touch both shores with our hands at the same time, while the average depth of water in the channel did not exceed five inches.

" Every paddle stroke seemed to increase the ardor with which we were carried forward. The desire to see the actual source of a river so celebrated as the Mississippi, whose mouth had been reached by La Salle nearly two centuries before, was doubtless a controlling incentive. What had long been sought at last appeared suddenly. On pulling and pushing our way through a network of rushes similar to the one encountered on leaving Itasca, the cheering sight of a transparent body of water burst upon our view. It was a beautiful lake— the source of the Father of Waters.

" A few moments later and our little flotilla of three canoes was put in motion, headed for a small promontory which we discerned at the opposite end of the lake. . . .

" As we neared the headland a deer was seen standing on the shore, and an eagle swept over our heads with food for its young, which we soon discovered were lodged in the top of a tall pine. The water-fowl noticed upon the lake were apparently little disturbed by our presence, and seldom left the surface of the water.

" This lake is about a mile and a half in greatest diameter, and would be nearly an oval in form but for a single promontory which extends its shores into the lake so as to give it in outline the appearance of a heart. Its feeders are three small creeks, two of which enter on the right and left of the headland, and have their origin in springs at the foot of sand-hills from two to three miles distant. The third inlet is but little more than a mile in length, has no clearly defined course, and is the outlet of a small lake situated in a marsh to the south-westward. These three creeks were named in the order of their discovery, Elk, Excelsior, and Eagle.

" Having satisfied myself as to its remotest feeders, I called my companions into line at the foot of the promontory which overlooks the lake, and talked for a few moments of the Mississippi and its explorers ; told them I was confident that we were looking upon the *true source* of the great river ; that we had completed a work begun by De Soto in 1541, and corrected a geographical error of half a century's standing. Concluding my remarks, I requested a volley from their firearms for each member of the party, in commemoration of our achievement. When the firing ceased, Paine gave me a surprise by stepping to the front and proposing ' that the newly discovered lake be named

Lake Glazier, in honor of its discoverer.' The proposition was seconded by Moses Lagard, the interpreter, and carried by acclamation."

Captain Glazier's biographer in "Sword and Pen" (pages 477, 478) here takes up the narrative:

"Standing then by the source of the mighty river, around which so many beautiful Indian legends cluster, and about which the white man has ever been curious, the captain felt a natural throb of pride that so much of his great undertaking had been successfully achieved, and a hope that the future held further good in store for him.

"Giving the order for embarkation, the canoes were soon gliding across the water, bound for Lake Itasca. Entering this lake, a short stop was made at Schoolcraft's Island in order to obtain the remainder of their luggage, after which they re-embarked, *at three o'clock in the afternoon*, and continued the descent of the river."

Thus it is shown from his own account that Captain Glazier spent less than twenty-four hours at Lake Itasca and in its vicinity; that the first sixteen hours of this brief day he made no attempt at any exploration; and that the time actually employed in finding the inlet of Lake Itasca, exploring its course to "Lake Glazier," returning to Schoolcraft's Island, and getting ready to start down the river for the Gulf of Mexico was only from 8 A.M. till 3 P.M.—seven hours—of the 22d of July, 1881. This, too, included the time occupied with the Captain's stump speech, the flight of the American eagle, and the drawing up of the petition "to the geographical societies" of the universe. Compare this exploit with Nicollet's three days *and nights* of devoted scientific research. Contrast the explorer of 1836, waiting seven years, and dying before his report was given to the world, with the adventurer of 1881, drawing up his petition for recognition before his actual work of exploration was yet seven hours advanced.

WHAT GLAZIER REALLY DISCOVERED.

But, however effectually Captain Glazier's claim to the discovery of the true source of the Mississippi may be disputed, no one will question one other claim that may be made in his behalf. Somewhere, somehow, Captain Glazier has discovered a copy of Mr. Schoolcraft's "Narrative of an Expedition to Lake Itasca in 1832."* And, as in the case of his discovery of "Lake Glazier," he imagined that he was the original and only discoverer and possessor of that work. Unfortunately for Captain Glazier, there are other copies of that work besides the precious one which he has "discovered."

Alongside of one of these other copies I desire to place Captain Glazier's account of his "Recent Discovery of the True Source of the Mississippi," as it appears in the "American Meteorological Journal" for 1884. Such a comparison will throw still further light on his claim to stand at the head of the long line of heroes of Mississippi exploration, from De Soto to Nicollet.

Mr. Schoolcraft and Captain Glazier did not follow the same route to Lake Itasca, but, from the junction of the Naiwa with the East Fork of the Mississippi, to Itasca Lake, their route was the same. Captain Glazier visited Leech Lake on his way to Itasca; Mr. Schoolcraft was at Leech Lake on his return from Itasca.

GLAZIER ON THE INDIAN QUESTION.

So, following Captain Glazier's order of procedure, we find the captain in 1881 on the spot where Mr. Schoolcraft had been in 1832, nearly fifty years before. They both found at this lake the headquarters of the Leech Lake, or Pillager, band of Chippewa Indians. Mr. Schoolcraft visited them at a time when they had but just come, in any real sense, under the care of the government. Mr. Schoolcraft was their agent, but his official residence was hundreds of miles away, at the eastern end of Lake Superior, and he had been in the region only once before, in 1820—before, indeed, he was appointed Indian Agent. When Captain Glazier visited Leech Lake, these Indians had been under the care of the government for fifty years. They had schools, saw-mills, grist-mills, wheat-fields, domestic animals; and though they were by no means the most progressive and civilized of the Chippewas, they were certainly not the untutored savages that Captain Glazier would have us imagine them to be.

But, bearing in mind what even a poor Indian policy can do for a tribe in fifty years, it is very well worth the while to com-

* Published by Harper & Brothers, New York, 1834.

pare the account of Glazier in 1884 with that of Schoolcraft in 1834:

"Schoolcraft's Narrative," 1834, p. 77.	*Glazier's Account,* "Am. Met. Journal," 1884, pp. 220, 221.
"This band appears to have separated themselves from the other Chippewas at an early day and to have taken upon themselves the duty which Reuben, Gad, and Manasseh assumed when they crossed the Jordan.	"This band seems to have separated from the other Chippewas at an early day and to have taken upon themselves the duty of defending this portion of the Chippewa frontier.
"They have ' passed armed before their brethren' in their march westward. Their geographical position is one which imposes upon them the defense of this portion of the Chippewa frontier. And it is a defense in which they have distinguished themselves as brave and active warriors. Many acts of intrepidity are related of them which would be recorded with admiration had white men been the actors.	"They 'passed armed before their brethren' in their march westward. Their geographical position was one which required them to assume great responsibilities, and in the defense of their chosen position they have distinguished themselves as brave and active warriors. Many acts of intrepidity are related of them which would be recorded with admiration had white men been the actors. . . . . .
"With fewer numbers the Chippewas have not hesitated to fall upon their enemies, and have routed them and driven them before them with a valor and resolution which in any period of written warfare would have been stamped as heroic. It is not easy on the part of the government to repress the feelings of hostility which have so long existed, and to convince them that they have lived into an age when milder maxims furnish the basis of wise action. Pacific counsels fall with little power upon a people situated so remotely from every good influence, and who cannot perceive in the restless spirit of their enemies any safeguard for the continuance of a peace, however formally it may have been concluded. This fact was adverted to by one of their chiefs, who observed that they were compelled to fight in self-defense. Although the Sioux had made a solemn peace with them at Tipisagi in 1825, they were attacked by them that very year and had almost yearly since sustained insidious or open attacks."	"With fewer numbers the Chippewas have not hesitated to fall upon their enemies, and have defeated and routed them with a valor and resolution which in any period of written warfare would have been stamped as heroic. It is not easy on the part of the government to repress the feelings of hostility which have so long existed, and to convince them that they have lived into an age when milder maxims furnish the basis of wise action. Pacific counsels fall with little power upon a people situated so remote from every good influence, and who cannot perceive in the restless spirit of their enemies any safeguard for the continuance of a peace, however formally it may have been concluded. The fact was adverted to by one of their chiefs, who observed that they were compelled to fight in self-defense. Although the Sioux had made a solemn peace with them at Tipisagi in 1825, they were attacked by them that very year and had almost yearly since sustained insidious or open attacks."

GLAZIER AS A PILLAGER.

And so Captain Glazier goes on for a page or more, *pillaging* the work of Mr. Schoolcraft. Can he be so benighted as not to know that fifty years have changed all this; that over twenty years ago the last Sioux was removed from Minnesota, and that half a million settlers and a million acres of wheat farms separate the Pillagers from their old enemies of the plains?

Yet Captain Glazier's eulogist in the "Sword and Pen" (pp. 448, 449) gives the above extracts from his private diary "as evidence of a certain power of philosophic reflection and inductive reasoning unusual in the mind of one so given to the excitement of an active and enterprising life as was Captain Glazier, who, as soldier, author, and explorer, certainly allowed himself little rest for the quiet abstractions of the student."

I differ with the eulogist, and submit that the above are very properly termed the "quiet *abstractions* of a student," and nothing else.

These "philosophic reflections" of Captain Glazier then proceed to take a survey of the domestic life and manners of the Pillagers and "all our Northern Indians," their nomadic life, "their want of domesticated animals, and *their general dependence on wild rice*" for subsistence, all of which must read very strangely to those acquainted with the Agency Indians of Minnesota. Then, adverting to their moral condition, these abstractions close as follows:

"Schoolcraft's Narrative," 1834, p. 80.	*Glazier's Account,* "Am. Met. Journal," 1884, pp. 221, 222.
"All that related to a system of dances, sacrifices, and ceremonies, which stood in the place of religion, still occupies that position, presenting a subject which is deemed the peculiar labor of evangelists. Missionaries have been *slow* to avail themselves of this field of labor, and it should not excite surprise that the people themselves are, to so great a degree, mentally the same in 1832 that they were on the arrival of the French on the St. Lawrence in 1532."	"All that related to a system of dances, sacrifices, and ceremonies, which stood in the place of religion still occupies that position, presenting a subject which is claimed to be the peculiar work of teachers and evangelists. Missionaries have been *seen* to avail themselves of this field of labor, and it should not excite surprise that the Chippewas are, to so great a degree, mentally the same in 1882 that they were on the arrival of the French in 1532."

GLAZIER *versus* MAJOR RUFFE.

Captain Glazier claims to have gained the above information from Major Ruffe, the Indian Agent at Leech Lake. If anything more is needed to show that these philosophic abstractions were at least fifty years behind the times, I would refer to the following extracts from Major Ruffe's report to the Indian Bureau under date of September 4, 1880:

" The uniform good conduct of the Indians under my charge, their civility toward each other, their generally correct deportment and freedom from indulgence in those vices peculiar to savages, and from which many civilized communities are not exempt, their evident desire to imitate what is thought best to conduce to their good and to eschew whatever seemed pernicious and evil, has characterized their social and moral habits, and merits most hearty commendation. No offense of a greater magnitude than a minor misdemeanor has been committed by any Indian within my jurisdiction, and even petty brawls or disorderly conduct have been of rare occurrence.

"An increasing interest has been manifested by the Indians in religious matters, and the efforts of zealous men devoted to their spiritual salvation have been rewarded by many proselytes, apparently sincere. . . . The attendance upon divine worship has increased in a gratifying degree, and the idolatrous practices of the savage have now become obsolete. . . .

"There are now 3,500 acres under cultivation, producing this year not less than 98,000 bushels of grain and vegetables, cultivated and harvested almost entirely by Indian labor. . . .

"The flour and saw mills upon this reservation are in good order and condition. . . . The mills in the Leech Lake and Red River Reservations are old, and unfit to meet the requirements of the respective localities. . . .

"An exposition of the products and industry of the Indians of this reservation was held here (at White Earth) last September. . . . I think I may safely say that few local industrial fairs presented a greater variety of domestic products, of superior workmanship and quality or excellence, than did the exposition of these Indians."

And this is the gentleman whom Captain Glazier credits with the statement that "the Chippewas are to so great a degree mentally the same in 1882 that they were on the arrival of the French in 1532."

But as early as the year 1836 to 1839 the Chippewas had improved far beyond where Captain Glazier would leave them even now. Here is the evidence of Mr. Nicollet:

"The territory of the Chippewas, the exploration of which I had just finished, as well as that of the Sioux, upon which I was entering, had been for many years tranquil. This is, beyond a doubt, to be attributed to the firmness of the Indian agents, Lieutenant Taliaferro and H. Schoolcraft, in enforcing the Law of 1832, prohibiting the introduction of ardent spirits, in which efforts they were warmly supported by Colonel Davenport, the commander of Fort Snelling, and Messrs. H. Sibley and Abm. Aitkin, agents of the American Fur Company. I found the same condition of things in 1837, 1838, and 1839, when the fort was under the command of Major Plympton; for during those years I continued to explore the vast region occupied by those two great nations. Then it was I bade a last adieu to the unconstrained liberty of the children of the forest, who, it requires no great foresight to anticipate, will soon have to yield to the restraints of civilization." *

And Charles Lanman, who visited Leech Lake in 1846, wrote of the Pillagers: †

---

* "Nicollet's Report." 1843, p. 66.
† Lanman's "Adventures in the Wilderness," vol. i., p. 79.

44 CAPTAIN GLAZIER AND HIS LAKE.

"They are good hunters, and pay more attention to agriculture than any other tribe of the [Chippewa] nation."

I do not believe any one will charge Major Ruffe with having so far traversed his official reports of the year before as to give Captain Glazier any such information as he credits to him. Major Ruffe was not a *Pillager*.

LEECH LAKE.

Both Mr. Schoolcraft and Captain Glazier were at Leech Lake, though fifty years apart, and it is not strange that they saw much the same characteristics of that peculiar body of water. Here is the way it looked to each of them :

"Schoolcraft's Narrative," 1834, p. 36.	Glazier's Account, "Am. Met. Journal," 1884. p. 219.
"Leech Lake is one of the most irregular shaped bodies of water that can be conceived of. It is neither characteristically long, spherical, or broad, but rather a combination of curves, . . . peninsulas, and bays, of which nothing short of a map can convey an accurate idea."	"Leech Lake is one of the most irregularly shaped bodies of water that can be conceived of. It is neither characteristically long, circular, nor broad, but rather a combination of curves, peninsulas, and bays, of which nothing short of a map can convey an accurate idea."

GLAZIER AND FLAT MOUTH.

At Leech Lake Mr. Schoolcraft accepted the invitation of "Aish Kibug Ekozh, the ruler of the Pillager band," to breakfast with him. Not to be outdone, Captain Glazier likewise accepted the invitation of "Flat Mouth, the present ruler of the Pillagers," to dinner. The accounts, when placed side by side, give us a graphic idea of the progress made in the past fifty years :

"Schoolcraft's Narrative," 1834, pp. 80, 81.	Glazier's Account, "Am. Met. Journal," 1884, pp. 222, 223.
"I went to his residence at the proper time, accompanied by Mr. Johnson. I found him living in a comfortable log-building of two rooms, well-floored and roofed, with a couple of small glass windows. *A mat was spread upon the center of the floor, which contained the breakfast. Other mats were spread around it to sit on. We followed his example in sitting down after the Eastern manner.*	"I went to his residence at the appointed hour, accompanied by my brother. I found him living in a comfortable log-house of two rooms, well-floored and roofed, with a couple of small glass windows. *A plain board table stood in the center of the front room, upon which the dinner was spread. Pine board benches were placed on each side of the table and at the ends. We followed the example of our host in sitting down.*
"There was no other person admitted to the meal but his wife, who sat near	"Five other persons, including his wife, were admitted to the meal. The

him, and poured out the tea, but ate or drank nothing herself. Teacups and teaspoons, plates, knives and forks of plain manufacture, were carefully arranged, and the number corresponding exactly with the expected guests. A white-fish, cut up and broiled in good taste, occupied a dish in the center, from which he helped us. A salt-cellar, in which pepper and salt were mixed in unequal proportions, allowed each the privilege of seasoning his fish with both or neither. Our tea was sweetened with the native sugar, and the dish of hard bread seemed to have been precisely wanted to make out the repast."

wife of Flat Mouth sat near him and poured out the tea, but ate or drank nothing herself. Teacups and teaspoons of plain manufacture were carefully arranged, the number corresponding exactly with the expected guests. A fine mess of bass and white-fish, cut up and boiled in good taste, occupied a dish in the center of the table, from which he helped us. A birch bark salt-cellar, in which pepper and salt were mixed in unequal proportion, allowed each the privilege of seasoning his fish with both or *either.* Our tea was sweetened with the native sugar. A dish of blue-berries picked on the shore of the lake completed the dinner."

Unfortunately, however, here again Mr. Nicollet comes in to the confusion of Captain Glazier, for in 1836 Mr. Nicollet enjoyed the hospitality of Esh Kebog Ikoj; and he found the amenities of social life on a much more liberal scale than did Mr. Schoolcraft in 1832. Nicollet says:

" During three successive evenings I went to take tea with Esh Kebog Ikoj, and drank it out of fine china-ware. . . . I need scarcely add, that these three long evenings spent with Esh Kebog Ikoj were full of instruction." *

It is not fair, however, to interrupt Captain Glazier in the midst of this banquet; and so, with an apology for the unwelcome intrusion of Nicollet, the description proceeds as follows:

"Schoolcraft's Narrative," 1834, p. 81.

" During the repast the room became filled with Indians, apparently the relatives and intimate friends of the chief, who seated themselves orderly and silently around the room. When we arose, the chief assumed the oratorical attitude, and addressed himself to me. " He expressed regret that I had not been able to visit them the year before, when I was expected. He hoped I had now come, as I came by surprise, to remain some days with them."

Glazier's Account, " Am. Met. Journal," 1884, p. 223.

" During the repast the room became filled with Indians, apparently the relatives and intimate friends of Flat Mouth, who seated themselves orderly and silently around. When we arose, White Cloud assumed the oratorical attitude, and addressed himself to me. " He expressed regret that his white brethren had been so long in ignorance of the source of the Mississippi. . . . He hoped I had come thoroughly prepared to explore the country beyond Lake Itasca."

Equally refreshing and instructive is the following compari-

---

* " Nicollet's Report," 1843, p. 62.

son of the character of Aish Kibug Ekozh, in 1832, with that of White Cloud in 1881:

"Schoolcraft's Narrative," 1834, pp. 81, 82.	Glazier's Account, "Am. Met. Journal," 1884, p. 223.
"This chief [Aish Kibug Ekozh], brought me a letter some years ago, at St. Mary's, in which he is spoken of as 'the most respectable man in the Chippewa country.' And if the term was applied to his mental qualities, and the power of drawing just conclusions from known premises, and the effects which these have had on his standing and influence with his own band, it is not misapplied. Shrewdness and quickness most of the chiefs possess, but there is more of the character of common sense and practical reflection in Guelle Plat's remarks than, with a very extensive acquaintance, I recollect to have noticed in most of the chiefs now living of this tribe.	"I was much gratified on this occasion by the presence of White Cloud, whom I had frequently been told was the most respectable man in the Chippewa country, and if the term was applied to his intellectual qualities, and the power of drawing just conclusions from known premises, and the effects which these have had on his standing and influence with his own tribe, it is not misapplied. Shrewdness and quickness of perception most of the chiefs possess, but there is more of the character of common sense and practical reflection in White Cloud's remarks than I remember to have noticed in most of the chiefs of my acquaintance.
"He is both a warrior and a counselor, and these distinctions he holds, not from any hereditary right, . . . but from the force of his own character. I found him ready to converse on the topics of most interest to him, and the sentiments he uttered . . . were such as would occur to a mind which had possessed itself of facts, and was capable of reasoning from them. His manners were grave and dignified, and his oratory such as to render him popular with his tribe."	"In his early life he was both a warrior and a counselor, and these distinctions he held, not from any hereditary right, but from the force of his own character. I found him quite ready to converse on the topics which were of most interest to him, and the sentiments he uttered were such as would occur to a mind which had possessed itself of facts and was capable of reasoning from them. His manners were grave and dignified, and his oratory such as to render him popular wherever heard."

AGAIN ON SCHOOLCRAFT'S TRAIL.

Captain Glazier again strikes the trail of Mr. Schoolcraft just before his arrival at Lake Itasca, and immediately he becomes graphic and scientific in his descriptions. It is where the River Naiwa joins the eastern branch of the Mississippi:

"Schoolcraft's Narrative," 1834, p. 52.	Glazier's Account, "Am. Met. Journal," 1884, pp. 258, 259.
"We found the channel above the Naiwa diminished to a clever brook, more decidedly marshy in the character of its shores, but not presenting in its plants or trees anything particularly to distinguish it from the lower part of the stream. The water is still and pond-like. It presents some small areas of wild rice. It appears to be a favorite resort for the duck and teal, who frequently rose before us, and were aroused again and again by our progress."	"We found the new stream more decidedly marshy in the character of its shores, but not presenting in its plants or trees anything to distinguish it particularly from the Naiwa. The water is still and pondlike. It presents some small areas of wild rice, and appears to be the favorite resort for the duck and teal, who frequently rose before us, and were aroused again and again by our progress."

And now they are both on their way up the eastern branch of the river, bound for Itasca Lake:

"Schoolcraft's Narrative," 1834, p. 52.	*Glazier's Account,* "Am. Met. Journal," 1884, p. 259.
"An hour and a half diligently employed brought us to the foot of Ossewa Lake. We halted a moment to survey it. It exhibits a broad border of aquatic plants with somewhat blackish waters. . . . It is the recipient of two brooks, and may be regarded as the source of this fork of the Mississippi. We were precisely twenty minutes in passing through it. We entered one of the brooks, the most southerly in position. It possessed no current, and was filled with broad-leaved plants and a kind of yellow pond-lily. We appeared to be involved in a morass where it seemed to be equally impracticable to make the land or proceed far by water. In this we were not mistaken. Oza Windib soon pushed his canoe into the weeds and exclaimed, '*Oma mikunna,*' ('here is a portage'). A man who is called on for the first time to debark in such a place will look about him to discover some dry spot to put his feet upon. No such spot, however, existed here. We stepped into rather warm pond water, with a miry bottom. After wading a hundred yards or more the soil became firm, and we soon began to ascend a slight elevation where the growth partakes more of the character of a forest. Traces of a path appeared here, and we suddenly entered an opening affording an eligible spot for landing. . . . The carbonaceous remains of former fires, the bones of birds, and scattered camp-poles proved it to be a spot which had previously been occupied by the Indians."	"Four hours of vigorous paddling brought us to the foot of a lake where we halted a few moments to survey. It exhibits a broad border of aquatic plants with somewhat blackish waters. It is the recipient of two brooks, and may be regarded as the source of this fork of the Mississippi. . . . We were twenty minutes in passing through the lake. . . . On reaching its southern end we entered one of the brooks. It possessed no perceptible current, and was filled with broad-leaved plants, rushes, and swamp grass. We appeared to be involved in a morass where it seemed impracticable to either make the land or proceed further by water. In this we were not mistaken. Che-no-wa-ge-sic soon pushed his canoe into the rushes and exclaimed, '*Oma mikunna*'—'here is the portage.' A man who is called on for the first time to debark in such a place will cast about for some dry spot to put his feet upon. No such spot, however, existed here. We stepped into rather warm pond water, with a miry bottom. After wading a hundred yards or more the soil became firm and we began to ascend a slight elevation where the growth partakes more of the character of a forest. Traces of a path appeared here, and we suddenly entered an opening which afforded an eligible place for landing. Remains of former fires, the bones of birds, and scattered camp-poles proved it to be a spot which had previously been occupied by the Indians."

MORE ORIGINAL DISCOVERIES.

Surely, such explorations as these are easy to make in the serene and quiet abstractions of the study. But the audacity of the following is beyond description:

"Schoolcraft's Narrative," 1834, p. 53.	*Glazier's Account,* "Am. Met. Journal," 1884, pp. 259, 260.
"Having followed out this branch of the Mississippi to its source, it may be observed that its existence as a separate river has hitherto been unknown in our geography. None of the maps indicate the ultimate separation of the Mississippi above Cass Lake into two forks."	"Having followed out this branch of the Mississippi to its source, it may be observed that its existence as a separate river has hitherto been unknown in our geography. None of the maps indicate the ultimate separation of the Mississippi above Lake Bemidji into two forks."

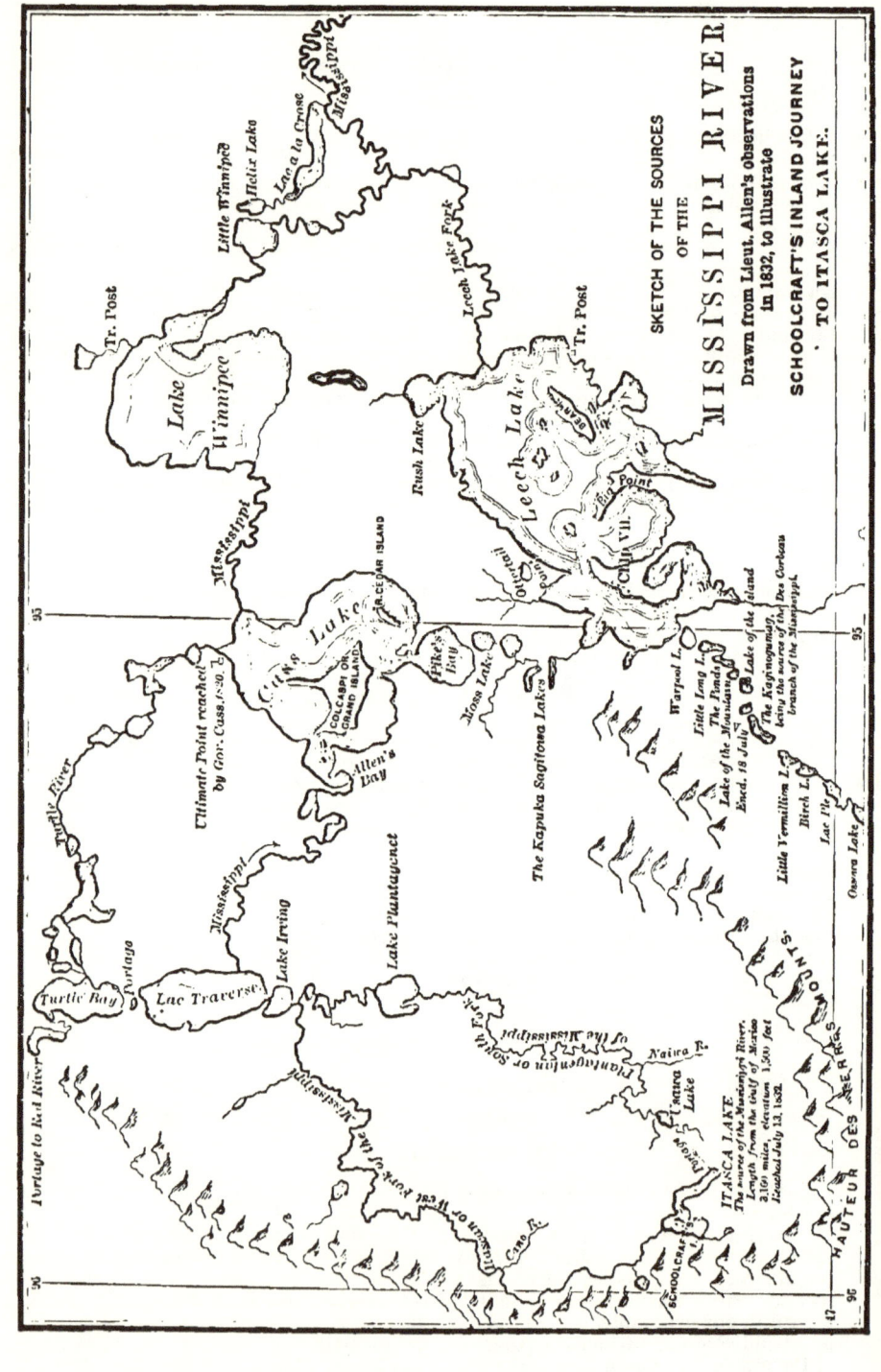

SKETCH OF THE SOURCES
OF THE
MISSISSIPPI RIVER
Drawn from Lieut. Allen's observations
in 1832, to illustrate
SCHOOLCRAFT'S INLAND JOURNEY
TO ITASCA LAKE.

If Captain Glazier will examine the volume of "Schoolcraft's Narrative" (edition of 1834), from which he copied the above, he will find, facing the title-page, a map of this whole region, on which is shown the entire course of this eastern fork. Where, indeed, did he get its course for his map if not there, or from some of the numerous map-makers who have copied from Schoolcraft? He does not pretend to have gone but a short part of its length. And now, as if to more thoroughly deceive his readers and the world, Captain Glazier thus pats the back of the man whose pockets he has just been engaged in rifling:

"I christened it Schoolcraft River, as a tribute to its discoverer, who, though he failed to reach the goal of his explorations, rendered valuable service in the department of geography."

This will not do. However much one may be disposed to honor Henry Rowe Schoolcraft, he will hardly care to do it under the lead of Captain Glazier. Furthermore, as I have before remarked, Mr. Nicollet was on that river fifty years ago; and he named it after his old and illustrious teacher, Laplace.*

But Captain Glazier is pushing forward to Lake Itasca:

"Schoolcraft's Narrative," 1834, pp. 53, 54.	*Glazier's Account,* "Am. Met. Journal," 1884, p. 261.
"The portage from the east to the west branch of the river is estimated to be six miles. Beginning in a marsh, it soon rises into a little elevation of white cedar wood, then plunges into the intricacies of a swamp matted with fallen trees, obscured with moss. From this the path emerges upon dry ground. It soon ascends an elevation of oceanic sand, having bowlders and bearing pines. There is then another descent and another elevation. In short, the traveler now finds himself crossing a series of diluvial sand-ridges which form the height of land between the Mississippi Valley and the Red River. It is, in fine, the table-land between the waters of Hudson's Bay and the Mexican Gulf. It also gives rise to the remotest tributaries of the River St. Louis, which, through Lake Superior and its connecting chain, may be considered as furnishing the head-waters of the St. Lawrence. This table-land is probably the highest in North-western America in this longitude."	"The portage from the eastern to the western branch of the Mississippi is six miles. Beginning in a marsh, it soon rises into a little elevation covered with a growth of cedar, white pine, and tamarack, then plunges into a swamp matted with fallen trees, obscured by moss. From the swamp the trail emerges upon dry ground, from whence it soon ascends an elevation of oceanic sand, having bowlders and bearing pines. There is then another descent and another elevation. In short, this portage carried us over a series of diluvial sand-ridges which form the height of land between the Mississippi and the Red River of the North. "These ridges constitute the table-land between the waters of Hudson's Bay and the Gulf of Mexico, and give rise to the remotest tributaries of the River St. Louis, which, through Lake Superior and its connecting chain, may be considered as furnishing the head-waters of the St. Lawrence. This is unquestionably the highest land of North America between the Alleghanies and the Rocky Mountains."

* "Nicollet's Report," 1843, p. 59.

4

Having thus indulged in a learned geographical diversion, for the benefit of his readers, the explorer again returns to the severer experiences of the trail:

"Schoolcraft's Narrative," 1834, p. 54.	Glazier's Account, "Am. Met. Journal," 1884, p. 261.
"In crossing this highland our Indian guide, Oza Windib, led the way, carrying one of the canoes as his part of the burden. The others followed, some bearing canoes and others baggage. The whole party were in Indian file and marched rapidly a distance, then put down their burden a few moments and again pressed forward. Each of these stops is denominated *Opugid-jiwunon*, or, a place of putting down the burden by the Indians. Thirteen of these rests are deemed the length of the portage. The path is rather blind, and requires the precision of an Indian eye to detect it. Even the guide was sometimes at a loss and went forward to explore. We passed a small lake, occupying a vale about midway of the portage, in canoes. The route beyond it was more obstructed with underbrush. To avoid this we waded through the margins of a couple of ponds near which we observed old camp-poles, indicating former journeys by the Indians."	"In crossing this highland my Indian guide, Che-no-wa-ge-sic, led the way, carrying, as usual, one of the canoes as his part of the burden. The others followed in Indian file, each bearing a canoe or its equivalent in luggage. As soon as all were on the trail we moved rapidly forward, halting occasionally for rest. The Chippewas denominate each of these stops *opugidjewunon*, or, a place of putting down the burden. Thirteen of these rests were given by Che-no-wa-ge-sic as the length of the portage. The trail is often obscured by a dense undergrowth, and requires the precision of an Indian eye to detect it. Even the guide was sometimes disconcerted and went forward to explore. About midway of the portage we came to a small lake, into which we quickly put our canoes and pulled for the opposite shore. The route beyond was more obstructed by underbrush. To avoid this we waded through the margins of a couple of ponds near which we observed old camp-poles, indicating former journeys by the Indians."

And now Captain Glazier, as if loath to leave this interesting region, regales his scientific readers in the "Meteorological Journal" with learned observations on the meteorology. zoology, and botany of this portage:

"Schoolcraft's Narrative," 1834, p. 54.	Glazier's Account, "Am. Met. Journal," 1884, pp. 261, 262.
"The weather was warm and not favorable to much activity in bird or beast. We saw one or two species of the *falco* and the common pigeon, which extends its migrations over the continent. Tracks of deer were numerous, but, traveling without the precaution required in hunting, we had no opportunity of seeing this animal on high grounds. . . . Ripe strawberries were brought to me by the men at one of the resting-places. I observed a very diminutive species of raspberry, with fruit, on the moist grounds. Botanists would probably deem the plants few, and destitute of much interest."	"The weather was much warmer than I had anticipated for this elevated region, and not favorable to much activity in bird or beast. Several flocks of pigeons and other birds common to northern latitudes were frequently observed. Tracks of deer were numerous in the marshes skirting the ponds, but, traveling without the precautions required in hunting, we had no opportunity of seeing this animal in the high grounds. Ripe strawberries were found on the hillsides, and a very small species of raspberry with fruit was brought to me by Che-no-wa-ge-sic at one of the resting-places. The students of botany would consider the plants few, and of little consequence."

Thus, treading in the very track and footprints of greatness, Captain Glazier reaches Lake Itasca. On the next day he paddles in his canoe a short distance up one of the feeders of Itasca and discovers "Lake Glazier." This is the way it happened:

"Schoolcraft's Narrative," 1834, pp. 55, 56.	Glazier's Account, "Am. Met. Journal," 1884, pp. 324, 325.
" Every step . . . seemed to increase the ardor with which we were carried forward. The desire of reaching the actual source of a stream so celebrated as the Mississippi— a stream which La Salle had reached the mouth of a century and a half (lacking a year) before—was perhaps predominant, and we followed our guides down the sides of our last elevation with the expectation of momentarily reaching the goal of our journey. What had been long sought at last appeared suddenly. On turning out of a thicket into a small weedy opening, the cheering sight of a transparent body of water burst on our view. It was Itasca Lake, the source of the Mississippi."	" Every paddle stroke seemed to increase the ardor with which we were carried forward. The desire to see the actual source of a river so celebrated as the Mississippi, whose mouth had been reached by La Salle nearly two centuries before, was doubtless the controlling incentive. . . . What had long been sought at last appeared suddenly. On pulling and pushing our way through a network of rushes similar to the one encountered on leaving Itasca, the cheering sight of a transparent body of water burst upon our view. It was a beautiful lake—the source of the Father of Waters."

This outburst of enthusiasm lasts but a moment, and the gallant captain again becomes the philosopher and scientist:

"Schoolcraft's Narrative," 1834, p. 58.	Glazier's Account, "Am. Met. Journal," 1884, p. 327.
" The height of this lake (Itasca) above the sea is an object of geographical interest, which, in the absence of actual survey, it may subserve the purposes of useful inquiry to estimate. From notes taken on the ascent it cannot be short of 160 feet above Cass Lake. Adding the estimate of 1,330 feet submitted in 1820 as the elevation of that lake, the Mississippi may be considered to originate at an altitude of 1,490, say 1,500, feet above the Atlantic. Its length, assuming former data as the basis and computing it through the Itascan or west fork, may be placed at 3,160 miles."	"Its (Lake Glazier's) height above the sea is an object of geographical interest, which, in the absence of actual survey, it may subserve the purposes of useful inquiry to estimate. From notes taken during the ascent it cannot be less than three feet above Lake Itasca. Adding the estimate of 1,575 feet, submitted by Schoolcraft in 1832 as the elevation of that lake, the Mississippi may be said to originate in an altitude of 1,578 feet above the Atlantic Ocean. Its length, taking former data as the basis, and computing through the western fork, may be placed at 3,184 miles."

And finally Captain Glazier takes leave of his readers of the "Meteorological Journal" with a philosophic piece of reasoning, which he thought to be so fine that he also incorporates it into his letter to the Secretary of the Royal Geographical Society. Accounting for the fact that the source of the Mississippi had not before been discovered, he says:

"Schoolcraft's Narrative," 1834, p. 59.	*Glazier's Account,* "Am. Met. Journal," 1884, p. 327.
" Its origin in the remote and unfrequented area of country between Leech Lake and Red River, probably an entire degree of latitude south of Turtle Lake, which still figures on some of our maps as its source, throws both the forks of this stream out of the usual route of the fur trade, and furnishes, perhaps, the best reason why its actual sources have so long remained enveloped in obscurity."	" Its origin in the remote and unfrequented region of country between Leech Lake and Red River, not less than an entire degree of latitude south of Turtle Lake, which was for many years regarded as the source, throws both forks of the stream out of the usual route of the fur traders, and furnishes the best reason, perhaps, why its fountain-head has remained so long enveloped in obscurity."

A FINAL "ABSTRACTION."

Then, as an "addendum" to his story of exploration, the Captain gives a "Summary of meteorological observations at the head-waters of the Mississippi," in which he records the state of the thermometer several times daily, and notes the condition of the sky, the direction and character of winds, etc., from July 17, to August 2, inclusive. It is interesting to compare these observations with those taken by Schoolcraft at Big Sandy Lake, and on the trip down the river from that lake to St. Peter. The original record is to be found in two tables on pages 268 and 314 of Schoolcraft's "Narrative of an Expedition to the Sources of the Mississippi in 1820," published in Albany, N. Y., in 1821 ; and these tables are condensed into one and appear in the form in which Glazier appropriates them, on page 423 of Schoolcraft's "Summary Narrative," published in 1855. The tables of Schoolcraft and Glazier are identical in every essential particular. The observations begin and end at the same day and hour. And why does Captain Glazier close his observations at 7 A.M. on the 2d of August, 1881? Because, just sixty-one years before, namely, on the 2d day of August, 1820, Mr. Schoolcraft, in attempting to take his usual observation at 2 o'clock P.M., broke his instrument, and therefore had to suspend his regular record of temperature for that day and for the balance of the journey. Such is the far-reaching influence of a seemingly trivial and unimportant circumstance !

The two tables are to be seen together on the following page.

Such is the case which Captain Glazier makes out against himself. If it throws discredit upon his whole story, and leaves the reader in doubt, whether, indeed, he ever saw Lake Itasca, he has no one save himself to blame.

[From " Schoolcraft's Summary Narrative," p. 423.]

Observations on the Sources of the Mississippi River.

	5 A.M.	7 A.M.	8 A.M.	12 M.	2 P.M.	8 P.M.	9 P.M.	REMARKS.
July 17	..	..	..	76°	80°	79°	78°	Morning rainy, then fair.
" 18	..	..	51°	64	66	53	50	Fair.
" 19	..	..	46	63	70	55	..	Night rainy, morning cloudy, then fair.
" 20	..	..	60	80	84	75	..	
" 21	..	..	68	86	88	85	74	
" 22	..	..	73	88	90	77	..	Cloudy, some thunder.
" 23	..	..	70	82	88	78	..	Night and morning rain, after-noon thunder.
" 24	..	..	74	87	80	78	..	Fair.
" 25	..	..	..	..	85	74	..	Fair.
" 26	61°	..	..	..	81	61	..	Morning fair, evening cloudy and rain. clear.
" 27	62	..	..	..	80	75	..	Morning fair, evening fair.
" 28	62	..	..	..	76	61	..	Morning fair, rain in afternoon.
" 29	50	..	..	..	74	52	..	Clear.
" 30	..	60°	..	..	76	..	63	Wind N.W., weather clear.
" 31	..	65	..	..	81	..	69	Wind W., weather clear.
Aug. 1	..	67	..	..	83	70	..	Fair.
" 2	..	72	..	..	*	..	..	Fair.

* Broke instrument.

[From *Glazier's Account*, " Am. Met. Journal," 1884, p. 328.]

Meteorological Observations at the Head-waters of the Mississippi.

	5 A.M.	7 A.M.	8 A.M.	12 M.	2 P.M.	8 P.M.	9 P.M.	REMARKS.
July 17	..	..	..	76°	80°	79°	78°	Morning rainy, then fair.
" 18	..	..	51°	64	66	53	50	Fair.
" 19	..	..	46	63	70	55	..	Night rainy, morning cloudy, then fair.
" 20	..	..	60	80	84	75	..	
" 21	..	..	68	86	88	85	74	
" 22	..	..	73	88	90	77	..	Cloudy, some thunder.
" 23	..	..	70	82	88	78	..	Night and morning rain. after-noon thunder.
" 24	..	..	74	87	80	78	..	Fair.
" 25	..	..	..	..	85	74	..	Fair.
" 26	61°	..	..	..	81	61	..	Morning fair, evening cloudy and rain, clear.
" 27	62	..	..	..	80	75	..	Morning fair, evening fair.
" 28	62	..	..	..	76	61	..	Morning fair, rain in afternoon.
" 29	50	..	..	..	74	52	..	Clear.
" 30	..	60°	..	..	76	..	63	Wind N.W., weather clear.
" 31	..	65	..	..	81	..	69	Wind W., weather clear.
Aug. 1	..	67	..	..	83	70	..	Fair.
" 2	..	72	..	..	..	..	..	Fair.

WHAT GLAZIER MIGHT HAVE DONE.

There is sufficient reason, however, to believe that Captain Glazier went to Lake Itasca and Elk Lake very much in the way and by the route he describes in his papers in the " Meteorological Journal," and certainly the projecting and carrying out of such a trip is, upon its face, highly creditable to any man. But it is not creditable to a professed explorer that he should be so utterly ignorant as was Captain Glazier, of the very simplest facts regarding the geography of the country he attempts to explore.

Captain Glazier should have fully informed himself regarding the work of Nicollet. Instead, he seems to have only the very vaguest notion of such a character.

He should have sought the help of the records in the Land Department at Washington. He evidently was not aware that there was such a department of the government.

He should have consulted the Topographical or Engineers' Bureau of the United States Army, where Nicollet's papers and note-books are deposited. Perhaps he did not know there was any such thing as a United States Army left after he resigned his commission.

At St. Paul he should have availed himself of the resources of the State Geological and Natural History Survey; then, and for a year or two before, in active study of the very region for which he was bound.

There, also, he should have consulted the officers, the library, and the valuable collection of papers of the Minnesota State Historical Society.

At St. Paul and Minneapolis he would have found a number of intelligent and courteous gentlemen in the Land Department of the Northern Pacific Railroad, who could have given him many hints as to what was known and what was to be discovered about the sources of the Mississippi.

The Register of the United States Land Office at St. Paul would have shown him the official plats of all the surveyed townships in the Itascan region, if he had but asked the privilege of consulting them.

Finally, he might have found the men who spent four weeks in September and October, 1875, making the government survey of the two townships which contain all the feeders of Elk Lake and Lake Itasca; and they would gladly have aided him with practical suggestions as to what to look for and where to find it.

All these sources of information are freely and cordially at the service of any intelligent explorer; and Captain Glazier would have gained a much larger opinion of the general intelligence of the American people if he had taken pains to find out how much is really known about the head-waters of the Mississippi, though his conceit of his own knowledge and importance might have suffered correspondingly.

And after such intelligent study of the problem, he would have found that there were still questions worthy the labors of a competent and properly equipped explorer. To the solution of these questions he should have addressed himself if he wished to add anything to the stock of knowledge concerning the great watershed of the height of land, and the drainage basin of Lake Itasca. This much is certain, that to see Elk Lake and Lake Itasca was not enough to compensate for the expense and trouble of going to the head-waters of the Mississippi.

THE REAL EXPLORATION OF THE ITASCA BASIN.

It is impossible to say how many exploring parties of white men had been to both those lakes before Captain Glazier, but there were, probably, a dozen or a score, at the least. They each could tell much of interest regarding that region, but it is safe to say that only two have added anything material to what Schoolcraft told the world in 1832. These two are the Nicollet Expedition of 1836, and the Land Department Surveyors of 1875. And we cannot too carefully note the different ways of working of these two explorations.

Nicollet was a trained scientist, but he worked under limitations, and very sensibly, also, with a limited and definite purpose. His work was mainly done alone, and his chief instruments were the thermometer, the barometer, the sextant, and the compass. Hence he gives us details of temperature, elevation, latitude, longitude, and the general direction of the parts he visited. He rarely used the chain, if, indeed, he carried such a piece of property. His details of distance were either estimated—as in the case of a day's tramp or an object within sight—or figured out by mathematical rules, as when he computed the length of a section of the river from the data of the latitude, longitude, and direction from each other of a given number of points in its course. Hence his outline of the course of a river or creek, or of the form of a lake or pond, was only as accurate as might be expected from a trained explorer, whose eye was accustomed to take in and measure distance, direction, and form, on a large scale, and under a thousand varying conditions. In the matter of general relief forms, and the general trend and drainage of the country, he was, without doubt, the best equipped and most competent single explorer who has undertaken the study of our country; and his work has been of inestimable value to hundreds of thousands who never heard of his name. So far as relates to the subdivision of areas, and the surveying and platting of the surface of the land, considered as a horizontal plane, his work did not profess to have any accuracy or value whatever.

On the other hand, this last is the chief, if not the only, object of the Government Land Surveyors. Their instructions are limited and specific. They take no note whatever of relief forms, they follow up and trace only the streams and ponds intercepted by the boundary-lines of sections. In the matter of horizontal area, in the meandering of lakes and navigable streams, and in the general platting of the land, they are proverbially reliable; but there is absolutely no account taken of elevation, and the drainage or trend of the land can only be inferred from the course and direction of the streams encountered in running the section lines.

Nicollet's exploration was made in 1836, before a surveyor's stake had been set within the limits of Minnesota. The Government Surveyors of 1875 perhaps never heard of Nicollet, and certainly had no thought of supplementing or verifying his work.

WHAT REMAINS TO BE DONE.

In general, therefore, the best sort of work that can be done by the explorer of to-day is to reconcile and adjust these two sets of data to each other. And, as applied to the head-waters of the Mississippi, the main thing to do is to determine and locate the exact water-shed which separates the Itasca basin from the sources of the Red River of the North on the one hand, and from the head-springs of tributaries of the Mississippi on the other.

Having definitely outlined the drainage basin to the south of Itasca, it is worth while to trace the principal feeders of the lake to their springs, to determine the area drained by each, the volume of their flow, and the rapidity of their currents, to measure the elevation of their extreme sources above the level of Lake Itasca, and to find how far they are perennial, and how much of their course is dry during a portion of the year. Investigation will also show what changes have occurred in the amount of natural water-supply in this region ; what alterations in the levels and dimensions of lakes and ponds have been occasioned by the choking up of their inlets or outlets by natural causes, or by the operation of beavers and other animals ; and whether any of the lakes or marshes are drained at any time by both the Mississippi and the Red River of the North. It will not take long, also, for an intelligent explorer to satisfy himself whether, at any time, Elk Lake and Itasca Lake were a continuous body of water connected by a broad channel.

These are some of the questions to which the future explorer should address himself, and such questions are the only ones whose investigation will justify any one in considering himself an explorer, or his work entitled to the consideration of geographers and geographical societies. It is, at the same time, safe to venture the prediction that the more thorough the investigation of the Itasca basin, the clearer will be the conclusion that Lake Itasca is the first considerable gathering-place of the great flood of waters which goes to make up the Mississippi River ; that Nicollet's rivulet, with its chain of three lakes, is, indeed, its most important feeder and principal tributary, and that it is still entitled to be called, as heretofore, the head and source of that mighty stream—Captain Glazier and his lake to the contrary notwithstanding.

FINALLY.

Already the settler is taking up land and felling timber on the shores of Lake Itasca ; and with the clearing of the forests, and the systematic drainage and cultivation of farms, the smaller streams and ponds will dry up and disappear, while other lakes and creeks will cease to have the importance that they may now possess. These changes, however, cannot affect the shape and conformation of the basin of Lake Itasca, or the location of the water-shed of the heights of land. There are certain elements in the region that are permanent, and certain others that are temporary and will soon undergo the changes which accompany the settlement and subjection of the wilderness. The Lake Itasca of Schoolcraft and Nicollet, in the main, survives to the present day. A few years more will see many of its features changed past recognition.

This, then, is an especially fitting time to supplement the work of Nicollet and the Government Surveyors, by a careful examination of the Itascan basin in the light of all previous explorations. If it is worth doing, it should not long be delayed; and that it is well worth doing, the interest of the public already enlisted in this discussion clearly proves. Further, the fact that a mere superficial charlatan has been able to lead astray and befog the press and the scientific bodies of almost the entire country, East and West, is no small proof that it is desirable to settle all the questions at issue.

The publishers of this paper, Messrs. Ivison, Blakeman, Taylor & Co., have taken this view of the case; and, ever since the first issue was raised with Captain Glazier, they have been satisfied that nothing short of a thorough exploration of the region in question would satisfy them, as educational publishers, or justify them in making any changes in their geographical textbooks. They have, therefore, authorized the equipment and dispatch of a competent exploring party to Lake Itasca; and, while I write this paragraph, the party is already on the ground with adequate force, and fully equipped with instruments for the complete survey and delineation of the region which supplies the chief feeders of Lake Itasca.

The results of this exploration will be thoroughly sifted, and it is reasonable to predict that they will be of such a character as to satisfy every one as to the exact conformation of the region which gives birth to the great Mississippi. Whatever may be learned will be given to the public as soon as it can be put in shape, and it is reasonable to expect that this too much vexed question will thus be finally and conclusively settled.

HENRY D. HARROWER.

753 BROADWAY, NEW YORK, *October* 20, 1886.

FOR SECONDARY SCHOOLS.

HISTORY.

Fisher's Outlines of Universal History.
Designed as a text-book and for private reading   1 vol., 8vo, 690 pages, 32 maps.   For introduction, $2.40.
"The best work of its kind extant in English."— *New York Tribune.*

Swinton's Outlines of the World's History
12mo, Illustrated, map, 500 pages.   For introduction, $1.44.

PHYSICS AND CHEMISTRY.

Cooley's New Text-Book of Physics.
By LeRoy C. Cooley, Ph.D. Revised. 12mo, 246 pages. Illustrated.
                                             For introduction, $0.90.

Wells's Natural Philosophy.
1 vol., 325 pages. Illustrated.   For introduction, $1.15.

Cooley's New Text-Book of Chemistry.
12mo, 303 pages, Illustrated.   For introduction, $0.90.

Eliot and Storer's Elementary Chemistry.
12mo, 359 pages, Illustrated.   For introduction, $1.08.

BOTANY.

Gray's How Plants Grow.
For young people and the schools. Small 4to, 500 Illustrations.
                                             For introduction, $0.80.

Gray's School and Field Book of Botany.
The most widely used botanical text-book in Secondary Schools. 8vo, 621 pages, Illustrated.   For introduction, $1.80.

Gray's Manual of Botany.
Eighth issue. Containing, besides illustrations, 20 plates of sedges, grasses, ferns, etc. 8vo, 700 pages.   For introduction, $1.62.

Gray's Structural Botany.
Being Vol. I. of Gray's New Botanical Text-Book.
                                             For introduction, $2.00.

Goodale's Physiological Botany.
Being Vol. II. of Gray's New Botanical Text-Book. (Vols. III. and IV. in preparation.)   For introduction, $2.00.

Coulter's Manual of the Botany of the Rocky Mountains.
For the use of Schools and Colleges between the Mississippi River and the Rocky Mountains. By Prof. John M. Coulter, Ph.D., Wabash College. 8vo, cloth, 496 pages.   For introduction, $1.62.

Gray and Coulter's Text-Book of Western Botany.
Consisting of Coulter's Manual of the Rocky Mountains, to which is prefixed Gray's Lessons in Botany.   For introduction, $2.16.

ZOOLOGY.

Tenney's Natural History of Animals.
By Sanborn Tenney and Abby A. Tenney. Illustrated with 500 wood engravings, chiefly of North American animals. Cloth, 12mo, 298 pages.
                                             For introduction, $1.20.

Tenney's Elements of Zoology (New).
Illustrated by over 750 wood engravings. 1 vol., cloth, 503 pages.
                                             For introduction, $1.60.

Tenney's Manual of Zoology.
Illustrated with over 500 engravings. Revised. For introduction, $2.00.

GEOLOGY.

Dana's Geological Story Briefly Told.
By Professor James D. Dana, LL.D. 1 vol., 12mo, 275 pages. Numerously illustrated and handsomely bound.   For introduction, $1.15.

Dana's New Text-Book of Geology.
Revised and enlarged. Illustrated by 450 engravings. 412 pages.
                                             For introduction, $2.00.

Dana's Manual of Geology.
Thoroughly revised, much enlarged, and almost wholly rewritten. Illustrated by over 1,150 figures in the text, 12 plates, and a physiographic chart of the world in colors. 1 vol., 8vo, cloth, 910 pages.
                                             For introduction, $3.84.

PHYSICAL GEOGRAPHY.

Guyot's Physical Geography.
By Arnold Guyot, late Blair Professor of Physical Geography and Geology, College of New Jersey. Large 4to, fully illustrated, charts, colored maps, etc. Full cloth, 124 pages. Revised, with new plates and newly-engraved maps.   For introduction, $1.60.

☞ Samples of any of the above sent for examination on receipt of price named.
☞ Our Brief Descriptive Catalogue sent Free on request.

IVISON, BLAKEMAN, TAYLOR, & CO., Publishers,
753 and 755 BROADWAY, NEW YORK.

WEBSTER'S
CONDENSED DICTIONARY.

Over 1,500 Illustrations.   Over 800 Pages.

Containing an adequate treatment of about 60,000 words of the English Language.

WEBSTER'S CONDENSED DICTIONARY is a thoroughly new individual work, based on the latest edition of the Unabridged Dictionary, but introducing many new features peculiar to itself.

THE CONDENSED DICTIONARY is an **American Book,** and contains every word in common use which, by any good and proper authority, is entitled to a place in a popular dictionary for American scholars and readers.

IN ITS ETYMOLOGIES the Condensed Dictionary can be compared to no other similar work save Webster's Unabridged. Being the most recent dictionary published, and every authority available having been exhausted in its preparation, it is safe to say it is most reliable in this important department.

IN THE MATTER OF DEFINITIONS Webster has always easily led every other authority, and this latest work of the Webster series is characterized by the same general superiority.

IN PRONUNCIATION the Condensed is especially clear and successful. The phonic markings are few and precise in their character, and every leading word is re-spelled phonetically.

THE SPELLING is strictly Websterian—a system which has steadily gained in favor and use until its leading features are now followed more generally than all other authorities throughout the English-speaking world.

THE CONDENSED DICTIONARY is for sale by all booksellers, and will be mailed, postpaid, to any address on receipt of $1.80.

IVISON, BLAKEMAN, TAYLOR, & CO., Publishers,
NEW YORK AND CHICAGO.

Important Announcement.

NOW READY.

AN INTERMEDIATE SERIES OF

SWINTON'S
READERS,

CONSISTING OF

Swinton's Advanced First Reader:

On the same plan as Swinton's Primer and First Reader; developing and extending the language work of that book. 120 pages.

Swinton's Advanced Second Reader:

On the plan of the Second Reader, with similar exercises in great variety. 176 pages.

Swinton's Advanced Third Reader:

With exercise in reading and language work similar to those of the Third Reader. 240 pages.

Swinton's Advanced Fourth Reader:

Composed (like the Fourth Reader) of new and interesting matter, largely original, for this important grade of school work. 384 pages.

The prices of these books are the same as those of corresponding grades of the regular series. A set of the four books sent, postpaid, on receipt of **$1.00.**

IVISON, BLAKEMAN, TAYLOR, & CO., Publishers,

NEW YORK AND CHICAGO.

STANDARD TEXT-BOOKS.

PRIMER OF PHYSIOLOGY AND HYGIENE

AND

ELEMENTARY PHYSIOLOGY AND HYGIENE.

By WILLIAM THAYER SMITH, M.D.,

Dartmouth Medical College.

MOST WIDELY ADOPTED.
UNIVERSALLY APPROVED.
THOROUGHLY SCIENTIFIC.

Strictly adapted to meet all the requirements of Recent Temperance Legislation.

THE PRIMER is designed for youngest classes. *Price for Examination and Introduction,* **30 cents.**

THE ELEMENTARY is designed for upper grammar classes and ungraded schools. *Price for Examination and Introduction,* **50 cents.**

AN IMPORTANT NEW BOOK.

THE PRINCIPLES OF HYGIENE.

Including the essentials of Anatomy and Physiology. For Schools. By EZRA M. HUNT, A.M., M.D., Sc.D., Tenth President of the American Public Health Association ; Secretary of the State Board of Health of N. J.; Instructor in Hygiene in the State Normal School of N. J. 12mo, cloth, illustrated, 400 pages.

This is an authoritative work, on an original plan, which makes the knowledge of Hygiene and the practice of its principles the first aim, using the study of Anatomy and Physiology as a means to this end, and not the end itself. The effects of alcoholic stimulants and narcotics are treated in proper connections, and the author has not failed to state the entire truth on these subjects and has been particular to give no doubtful views.

PRICE BY MAIL, $1.00.

Our Descriptive List Sent Free to any address on request.

IVISON, BLAKEMAN, TAYLOR, & COMPANY,

EDUCATIONAL PUBLISHERS,

149 WABASH AVE., CHICAGO.   753 AND 755 BROADWAY, NEW YORK.

SWINTON'S SIXTH

OR

Classic English Reader.

An Advanced Number in the well-known series of School Reading Books, by WM. SWINTON.

DESIGNED FOR THE UPPER GRADES OF GRAMMAR SCHOOLS, AND FOR HIGH SCHOOLS, ACADEMIES, AND SEMINARIES.

Containing representative selections from the writings of ten British and ten American authors, chronologically arranged, with critical sketches of the Life and Works of each, with annotations.

AUTHORS.

SHAKESPEARE.	WEBSTER.	WHITTIER.
MILTON.	IRVING.	POE.
ADDISON.	BYRON.	HOLMES.
POPE.	BRYANT.	TENNYSON.
FRANKLIN.	MACAULAY.	THACKERAY
BURKE.	EMERSON.	LOWELL.
SCOTT.	LONGFELLOW.	

By its method and scope the Classic English Reader not only provides a manual for advanced classes in keeping with the high character of the general series, but also forms, with its biographical and critical notes, a sterling text-book of English Literature.

Cloth, 16mo. 608 pages. Sent, postpaid, for examination with a view to introduction, on receipt of $1.00.

Swinton's New Readers,

Numbers One, Two, Three, Four, and Five, form a complete series for schools, and combine the most approved methods, an excellent course of language training, selections of high literary value, and unsurpassed mechanical and artistic execution.

The Set for Examination, $1.75.

IVISON, BLAKEMAN, TAYLOR, & CO.,

753 and 755 Broadway, NEW YORK. 149 Wabash Ave., CHICAGO.

"THE COMMON BRANCHES."

The attention of Teachers and School Officers is invited to our very complete list of publications, comprising not only well-known Standard Text-Books in every branch of study, but many new and highly popular works in the "common branches." Among the latter are:

READING.—SWINTON'S SERIES.
Five Books, and a sixth, or Classic English Reader. Also "Swinton's Advanced Readers." Four Books.

SPELLING.—SWINTON'S WORD BOOKS.
Spelling and Word Analysis.

ARITHMETIC.—FISH'S SERIES. Two Books.

GEOGRAPHY.—SWINTON'S SERIES. Two Books.

GRAMMAR.—WELLS'S SHORTER COURSE. One Book.

HISTORY.—SWINTON'S CONDENSED UNITED STATES.
One Book.

PENMANSHIP.—SPENCERIAN COPY-BOOKS.
Complete and Shorter Course.

*** Descriptive circulars, with full information about the many points of excellence claimed for these fresh and thoroughly prepared books, together with suggestions as to how they may be introduced at merely nominal prices, will be sent by mail on application.

REPRESENTATIVE STANDARD BOOKS.

Fisher's Outlines of Universal History.
Swinton's Outlines of the World's History.
Bryant and Stratton's Book-keeping.
Robinson's Mathematics.
Gray's Botany.
Dana's Geologies.
Guyot's Geographies.
Felter's Arithmetics.
The New Graded Readers.
Sheldon's Readers.
Kerl's Grammars.
Smith's Physiology and Hygiene.
Cooley's Chemistry and Physics.

Our Brief Descriptive Catalogue, containing more than 300 volumes, will be mailed free on application.

IVISON, BLAKEMAN, TAYLOR, & CO., Publishers,
753 and 755 Broadway, New York.

CAPTAIN GLAZIER

AND

HIS LAKE

An Inquiry

INTO THE HISTORY AND PROGRESS OF EXPLORATION AT THE
HEAD-WATERS OF THE MISSISSIPPI SINCE THE
DISCOVERY OF LAKE ITASCA

IVISON, BLAKEMAN, TAYLOR & COMPANY

NEW YORK AND CHICAGO

LOCAL GEOGRAPHY

SUCCESSFULLY TREATED IN

SWINTON'S GEOGRAPHIES.

For the convenience of schools, SWINTON'S GRAMMAR SCHOOL GEOGRAPHY is issued in **SIX SEPARATE EDITIONS**, each containing a supplement of from 30 to 40 pages, treating of the special geography of a group of States, thus making each edition complete in about 150 quarto pages, as follows:

I. NEW ENGLAND EDITION: With Supplement of 32 pages, containing special county, town, and railroad maps and descriptive geography of

MAINE,	VERMONT,	CONNECTICUT,
NEW HAMPSHIRE,	MASSACHUSETTS,	RHODE ISLAND.

II. MIDDLE STATES EDITION: With Supplement of 33 pages, containing special county and railroad maps and descriptive text of

..EW YORK,	PENNSYLVANIA,	DELAWARE,
NEW JERSEY,	MARYLAND,	DISTRICT OF COLUMBIA.

III. SOUTHERN STATES EDITION: With Supplement of 37 pages, embracing special county and railroad maps and full descriptive text of

VIRGINIA,	ALABAMA,	ARKANSAS,
WEST VIRGINIA,	FLORIDA,	TEXAS,
NORTH CAROLINA,	MISSISSIPPI,	KENTUCKY,
SOUTH CAROLINA,	LOUISIANA,	TENNESSEE.
GEORGIA,		

IV. EAST CENTRAL STATES EDITION: With Supplement of 33 pages, giving special county and railroad maps and full descriptive geography of

OHIO,	ILLINOIS,	WISCONSIN.
INDIANA,	MICHIGAN,	

V. WEST CENTRAL STATES EDITION: With Supplement of 40 pages, containing special county and railroad maps and descriptive text of

MINNESOTA,	MISSOURI,	NEBRASKA,
IOWA,	KANSAS,	DAKOTA.

VI. PACIFIC STATES EDITION: With Supplement of 42 pages, presenting county and railroad maps and full special text of

COLORADO,	MONTANA,	NEW MEXICO,
CALIFORNIA,	IDAHO,	ARIZONA.
NEVADA,	WYOMING,	WASHINGTON,
OREGON,	UTAH,	ALASKA.

SWINTON'S GRAMMAR SCHOOL GEOGRAPHY

proper, is a school text-book of 118 large quarto pages, treating of the general Geography of the World—*Physical, Political, and Commercial*. It is handsomely illustrated with a great number of engravings, and contains over *forty* pages of valuable Maps for study and reference.

SWINTON'S INTRODUCTORY GEOGRAPHY,

IN READINGS AND RECITATIONS, is a new work for primary classes, designed to be used as a preparatory book to the Grammar School Geography. The two form a most complete and satisfactory TWO-BOOK COURSE for all classes of public and graded schools.

*** *Correspondence relating to the introduction of Swinton's Geographies is cordially invited.*

IVISON, BLAKEMAN, TAYLOR, & CO., - New York and Chicago.

IT IS IMPOSSIBLE to advertise in detail all the works included in our extensive list, which now embraces several hundred carefully prepared text-books covering nearly every branch of study. Teachers should remember that whenever a change is desired it will pay them to open correspondence with us.

Swinton's Geographies meet the most exacting demands of the school-room. For examination the **Introductory** is sent for 35 cents and the **Grammar School** for 65 cents.

Swinton's Readers teach reading by the most approved methods; furnish perfectly graded selections; and contain a thorough course of language training.

Swinton's Advanced Readers in four numbers, supplement any series with the choicest reading matter.

Manson's Blanks for written spelling meet every demand. Sample for any grade sent free on request.

Fisher's Outlines of Universal History. The *New York Tribune* pronounces it "the best work of its kind extant in English"—and in this opinion the educators and critics concur. Send for circular.

Be Sure that you correspond with us before making any changes in books this fall.

Our Brief Descriptive List sent free to any address.

IVISON, BLAKEMAN, TAYLOR, & CO.,

753 and 755 Broadway, New York.

A Library Edition, in TWO VOLUMES, of

FISHER'S OUTLINES

OF

UNIVERSAL HISTORY.

By GEO. PARK FISHER, D.D., LL.D.,

OF YALE COLLEGE.

"It was a formidable task that the author undertook, and he has performed it in a manner worthy of all praise......It will be found to contain a survey of the entire field of history admirable for its breadth and insight."

N. Y. NATION.

"..I am astonished that any one man should have been able to write such a work as the 'Outlines of Universal History.' No living man is more competent to do it than Dr. Fisher. I keep the book on my table for constant reference."

President JAS. McCOSH, LL.D., Princeton College.

"..Brief, condensed, well arranged, luminous, impartial."

PHILLIP SCHAFF, S. T. D.

"..I have no hesitation in heartily indorsing and recommending it.."

FRANCIS BROWN, D.D., Union Theol. Sem.

"..Better than anything of its kind we have had heretofore.."

W. P. ATKINSON, Prof. Hist., Mass. Inst. Technology.

"..Decidedly the best work of its class.."

Prof. CHAS. F. RICHARDSON, Dartmouth Coll.

"..I cannot speak in terms of too high praise of the excellence of the work.."

Pres. J. B. ANGELL, Univ. of Mich.

"..Having no superior, and in some respects it has no equal.."

W. G. T. SHEDD, D.D., Union Theol. Sem.

"..It seems to me the best work of its kind.."

Pres. S. CLARK SEELYE, Smith Coll.

"..The best work of its kind in the English language.."

Prof. ANSON D. MORSE, Amherst Coll.

---

2 Vols., 8vo, Cloth, Large Paper, Uncut, Gilt Top, in box, $5.00.

IVISON, BLAKEMAN, TAYLOR, & CO.

753 and 755 Broadway, New York.